MAHISHAA
A LOVE STORY

by
MAHISHAASURA
As told to Lakshmi

 Vitasta

Published by
Renu Kaul Verma
Vitasta Publishing Pvt Ltd
2/15, Ansari Road, Daryaganj
New Delhi - 110 002
info@vitastapublishing.com

ISBN 978-93-90961-22-1

© Lakshmi Bayi
First Edition 2022
MRP ₹ 595

All Rights Reserved.

No part of this publication may be reproduced, stored in a retrieval system or transmitted in any form, or by any means—electronic, mechanical, photocopying, recording or otherwise—without the prior permission of the publisher.

Editor: Papri Sen Sri Raman
Layout and Cover Design: Somesh Kumar Mishra
Printed at Thomson Press (India) Ltd, New Delhi

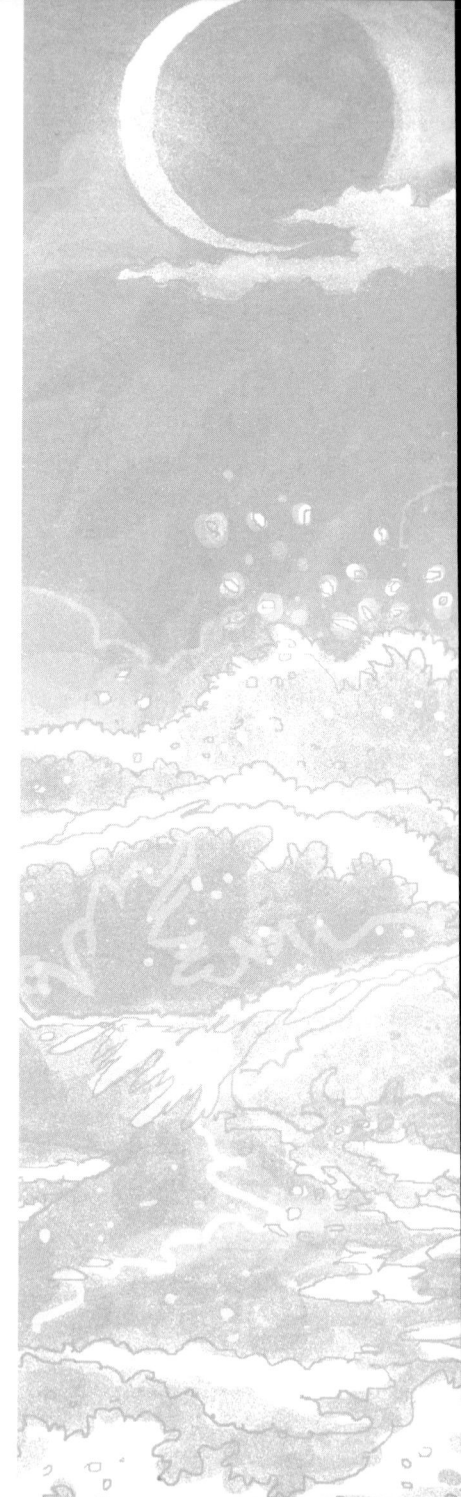

To
G M
*beyond Words
and Silences*

CONTENTS

XI PREFACE

1 KAALI
3 AND I, LAKSHMI
5 LOVE
7 SHIVA
11 ENTRE MAHISHAA
15 THEN CAME THE GODS
17 AND STORY TIME
81 LAKSHMI
121 MAHISHAALAKSHMI
129 MAHISHAASURA
167 KAAL
173 MAHAKAAL

181 GLOSSARY
185 ACKNOWLEDGEMENTS

Invocation

Why did You pretend to do penance for Him
When all along You had ordained Him for You?
Did You do it to pander to his male ego?
A fact and facet that is there for all males
Divine and otherwise.

There was only You before the beginning
There will only be You after the end
There was nothing without You
Nothing but You.
Yes, You are this bit of protoplasm too
That I refer to as 'I'.

Credit: Mahishaasuramardini, the Stone Sculpture form of Goddess Durga Slaying Demon Mahishaasura. This beautiful statue is displayed in the British Museum, London.

https://i.pinimg.com/.../feb4d8b5eb9835382671182069ead490...

THE POET

Kaali I am lost in a fixation
On your black skin
Which shines as if there were flames
Where your flesh touches the deepest
Layer of your skin.

How many wounds to your body do you bear,
Goddess with a fatally-wounded heart
That happened when you refused
Your adoring demon lover?

How many kisses you bore
From the icy lips of the
Dancing hermit of Kailasam?

How many nights were layered
One over the other
With stars appliqued to them
To get you that liquid shade of black?

How many sacred names will you acknowledge
Make them your own
Drawing in your breath sharply
Laughing and crying at
'Mahishaasuramardini'
The one name you respond to
First and most?

Preface

From the very first day of Creation, there has been a conflict between what is commonly named 'good' and 'evil'. These are merely two extreme ends of the spectrum of Existence, and this is required to bring out the various shades of Being in between.

This book is about various shades of interpersonal greys; no one is Black or White, we are all Greys. Its about an imperfect Devi who thinks she is meting out justice but realises how unfair She has been. It is about the mighty Mahisha king who realises despite his divine boons how vulnerable he is.

This is a tale of loneliness and the meeting of two lonely hearts. It is a story of desire, unfulfilled and of perceived incompatibility; no one asks the protagonists what they want. The story is a reflection of society where love is never factored in, in any normal and rational discussion of any of life's processes. This story teaches us that there is no ABSOLUTE good or TOTALLY bad. We are what we are, shades of GREY.

Irrespective of ethnicity, economics, language, diet, skin pigmentation etc all human beings (as well as all living beings) have an extra-physical dimension to them. Ironically, this is most evident at the point of death! Unlike sleep, which will result in wakefulness at the end of the cycle, death is an activity from which the only possible future is physical decomposition, which is handled by the living 'disposing off' the inert physical remains.

In simple biology we see the birth, growth, death and regeneration cycle in most creatures. Nature has Her own method of dealing with Her own systems in a way that cannot be bettered.

Human beings worldwide have claimed for themselves a supremacy in Nature. One of the main reasons for this is that there are no other species yet, who can counter this. So far, human beings are the only group that can store and retrieve their collected knowledge that can be used at will. This gives them a definite advantage over the rest of creation.

This huge knowledge bank has led to a collection of marvellous narratives. whether they are 'myths' or history is a point for scholars to endlessly argue about!

Human beings are not merely mechanical entities whose existence consists of conception, birth, growth and death. Beyond basic childhood, with its largely physical needs of feeding and sleeping, human beings become aware of a more complex 'inner' world. It is this part of human beings which graduates them into being artistes and scientists. Merely physical survival becomes inadequate. This search beyond the plane which can be made evident by the use of the Five Senses, becomes a spiritual quest.

This hungering for knowledge is again common throughout the world. In this journey, certain questions arise, answers are arrived at and collected.

Any group which adheres to a certain set of postulates becomes a sect or a religion. The 'boss' of such groups is invariably a superhuman being, commonly referred to as 'God'. The attributes of the Divinities may be different. There IS an unnamed, unknown, unmeasurable force in this World that makes the whole system work, which has its existence independent of whether its creations acknowledge it or not. But it is when human beings talk about that, that it is lowered into the mortal plane and seeks to add on very human attributes to it. For example, any person even casually observing a thunderstorm, can well understand, the creator behind it is unlikely to be contained by a merely human form!

But then, it is the very nature of human society to seek to 'define' everything in the most mundane of terms.

One of the earliest manifestations of this Divinity is that of the Mother Goddess. The act of giving birth is one which fills even today's experience-hardened doctors with a sense of wonder. Imagine the effect of this on primitive human beings! A birth passage, a womb and pendulous breasts to nourish the offspring were the attributes of a mother. This can be seen in primitive images, supposedly used in worship.

The mystery of death was offset by the miracle of birth and the Mother was a key player in this. She was crucial to keep adding to the species, especially at a time when numbers made a very big difference between survival and annihilation.

From this primal Goddess image, the rest of the clan of Divinities arise. This creating, nurturing female image can be seen throughout the religions of the world. It is indeed much later on that economic, social and political considerations tried to demote these Goddesses into auxiliary energy forms to unabashedly male deities.

A casual look at the female-male couples of international Divinities will indeed highlight the power of the female. Shiva-Shakthi, Osiris-Isis, Zeus-Hera, Jupiter-Hera, Odin-Frigg, Lakshmi-Narayana etc show the unbreakable link and interdependence of the female-male energies in the Universe. Except for some parthenogenetic creatures, a male and a female is required for creation. In almost all the cases, the narratives are cyclical and not linear in nature. In Maharashtra the Goddess kills Mhasoba, who is resurrected and then married to the Goddess. This idea of the very Kalpas coming again round and round is very prevalent in this country.

The female aspect of Energy is something which cannot be dismissed, let alone denied.

Shri Aadi Shankara's exquisitely layered 100 stanzas of the *Soundaryalahari*, or *Intoxication of Beauty* states thus in the opening paragraph itself:
Shiva Shakthya Yuktho Yadi Bhavathi Shaktha Prabhavithum
Na Che Devam Devo Na Khalu Kushala Spandithum Abhi.

Without the mingling of Shiva and Shakthi, there is no movement possible.

In Sanskrit language the word Shiva becomes 'Shaba' or corpse without the 'EE' ending. The 'E – kaaram' stands for Devi or the Female Energy.

Such is the importance of the Female Energy.

In the Indian context the manifestations of the Female Energy, variously known as Shakthi, Bhagavathi, Devi etc are manifold. She exists as the highly esoteric 'Bindu' or a dot, the flamboyant Lakshmi, whimsical bestower of good fortune and Her feared elder sister Alakshmi or Jyeshta, giver of misfortune.

The group of Ten and Seven special groupings of Goddesses are known as Dasha Maha Vidya and Saptha Matrkas respectively.

We have the well-known Trinity of Goddesses Saraswathi, Lakshmi and Parvathi who are the Deities of Wisdom, Wealth and Valour. Without these Three Qualities, there will be incompleteness in Life.

The snake-hooded Naageshwari exists alongside with the mongoose-faced Nakhudi. In fact Bahuchaarika, the patron Goddess of transgenders, with Her weapons and riding forth on a cock is as revered as the Nine Devis worshipped during Navarathri or the ancient Vedic deity, Usha or Dawn.

All these archaic texts extol the power of Nature. It is in the later texts that the Thirtythree Crore Gods, in Their wonderful variety, make their appearances.

Another striking similarity is that Goddess Kaali, the controller of Time, is depicted as both Nurturer and Destroyer.

'Bhadra Kaali Rudra Sutha' is the daughter of Shiva, as well as His spouse. This same linkage is found in the other stories from many places as well.

There are so many holy books in Sanatana Dharma. The Mahishaasuramardini Shloka in the Chandi Shathaka speaks of: *Kim Va Krishnaankhri Padma Dyuthibhirarutha Vishnu Padya Prapadyaa.* That Goddess whose dark Feet are lit up by the lights reflecting off the gem-encrusted crowns of the other Deities, supplicating to Her.

Shiva-purana places Shiva as the most powerful God of the pantheon, as does the *Vishnu-purana*, Hari, yet another name for Vishnu.

The *Durga Sapthashathi*, the *Shri Devi Bhaagavatham* etc are rich sources of the Divine Leela or play of the Mother Goddess. The great Vaishnavite love story between Krishna, the Ninth incarnation of Maha Vishnu and Shri Radha, His older lover is not depicted in the *Bhagavatham*, Veda Vyaasa's book on Krishna. Yet, Shri Radha finds great prominence in the *Shri Devi Bhagavatham*. It is Radha who is more often worshipped with Krishna than His official spouses (numbering sixteen thousand and eight), like Rukmini, Sathyabhama etc.

There are Nine different forms of Bhakthi or worship. They are Shravana (listening to holy things), Kirtana (singing about God), Smarana (remembering God), Pada-Sevana (worshipping God's Feet), Archana (worship), Vandana (to wish or show respect with folded hands), Dasya (to be a slave), Sakhya (to consider God to be a friend) and Atma Nivedana (complete surrender to God), which is often considered to be the highest form of Bhakthi.

In this book, *Mahishaasuramardini*, we see the genesis of Mahishaasura, what his motivations were, how he got to be where he was, and his relationship with the Goddess. Durga is the deity who in Bengal is associated with the killing of Mahishaasura, while Kerala has the Goddess killing the demon Daarika, a local version of the demon. 'Durga' is a word in Sanskrit that means 'fort' and also for the state of mind as well.

Kaali is clearly the Controller of Time. There are at least Nine versions of the Goddess Kaali. It is She who decides the timing of all events. A Goddess who decimated the demon Dhumralochan and his cohorts with a mere 'hoonkaar' or roar obviously does not require a protracted battle with Mahishaa to annihilate him.

When nothing matters to him more than the Devi, Mahishaa's battle turns magically into a love story.

This story deals with love, both physical and emotional which culminates in total surrender. Mahishaa is born out of the conjugation of an asura with a gentle beast. He is born with his mother's bovine head. Yet, during his emotional journey towards divinity, he uses his shape-shifting powers to woo Devi. At first, to frighten her, as she waits outside his gate, singing, he becomes a fierce Asura with a Asura head; then he adopts a buffalo shape, then he becomes a buffalo body with a love-lorn asura-human head. One generally finds the head that the Devi hunts and holds is this asura-human head. The Poet imagines Asura merging with Devi to become One in the throes of love.

The speciality of Sanatana Dharma is its endless capacity for being inclusive. There is a limitlessness and beauty to it which cannot be contained by, or conceived of, by mundane human beings. However, anyone with a smidgeon of understanding of the vastness of this ancient, vital way of Life, will be able to accept the position of Shiva as well as Mahishaa, in the story of the most fascinating of Goddesses, much beyond accepted Divinity to that Giver of Life, Love and ultimately, Salvation.

Kaali

Kaali was just one of the names given to the Mother Goddess. Some devotee gave Her this name. She gave us this story.

The solitary lamp on the eastern side of the temple was lit. It was an ancient one made of brass. Mani polished it so that it shone like antique gold. There were two wicks burning low, one to the east and the other to the west. Behind the temple there were granite steps leading down to the riverbank. The river shimmered in the full moon night like a silver snake mating with a black one.

Kaali sat on the top step. Her thick hair was unbound and it carried within the scent of flowers that do not grow on earth. The reddish tinge of kunkumam was there on Her forehead. Her third eye, with its luxuriant lashes looked like a designer pottu, bang in the middle of Her forehead. Her other two eyes were not visible; they looked like dark pools of infinity. Her nose was sharp and looked beautiful especially when Her profile was towards me. The lion and the elephant She wore in Her ears rumbled gently. Her lips were fragrant with the smell of

betel leaf. Her fangs showed up for a micro-moment like swords, ready to be impaled on the earth. She wore exquisite jewelry and the living snakes She wore twined themselves through the gems as if they were still hibernating in the mines below.

The garland of human skulls around Her neck chatted hollowly. Her soft hands bore the scars of the weaponry She wielded with ease. Her nails were sharp and blood red. She wore a loincloth of red silk with a broad gold border. Tiny golden bells rang out from Her anklet. By a feat of what seemed magic, there were thousands upon thousands of lamps glittering by Her feet. They were the *Lalitha Sahasranamam*s, prayers, petitions and desires of Her many worshippers.

Leaning back comfortably on the step She spoke. Her voice was like the monsoon wind rushing through the parched forests, waiting for a thorough drenching. As She spoke I listened riveted. I was no longer a bhaktha, a writer. I was sheer ectoplasm, part of what She was. I was Her.

And I, Lakshmi

'Energy cannot be created or destroyed. It can only change forms.'

That was eighth class physics for you, enunciated by a dark Goddess.

'I, you, all that we see around is just energy.'

'e=mc squared', I mutter, keen to show off my recall.

'Yes, this world is made out of energy', She said. 'Do you like it?'

I could sense rather than see Her smile.

'Sometimes.' I shrugged the way it used to irritate my family and teachers. It was a universal gesture of the so-called difficult ones. The ones who ask questions, and don't accept stock answers.

'I shall give you answers so that you can think up further questions', She said benignly. 'Let us get to know each other. Let me tell you my story.'

I loved stories.

'I am the first energy', She said. 'Huge. Diverse. Strong.'

'Neutral?' I add. That is what I had learned.

'No!' She was emphatic. 'I am love.'

I started laughing. That was such a cliché! Every marketer of fakes used it!

Her black hand caught hold of my wrist. It felt burning cold.

'I am Love', She said. 'It is only Love that created all the Gods, humans, the whole of creation. You are sitting with me now, is that not your love for stories, more than your bhakthi for me?'

It took a Goddess of that caliber to make me see that truth.

Love

'Love comes in many forms', Kaali said.

Still keen to show off, I muttered, 'Energy cannot be created or destroyed. But it can change forms.'

'Exactly! I prefer scientists who have no fuzzy logic, rather than the fake swamis who do atrocities in my name.' She was appreciative.

'It is not just the Hindu religious heads who misuse my name. The Christians, the Muslims – they all do it in the name of different Divinities. We are all different names of the same Almighty. Many a time, the fights are about property. Perceived power. Perceptions matter, not truth.'

'What are they then, the Christian Divinities and the single God of Islam?'

She answered my question with another of Hers.

'Why do you believe in me?'

'Because you are easy to deal with. You are beautiful, familiar. You are

Shakthi. Power. You protect your bhakthas, your children and you kill those who deal harm.'

There was a silence.

'You could be called user-friendly, I suppose', I said.

Her laughter rose from Her belly. It rang out like fast approaching thunder.

'Who told you all that?' Her voice was tender, joking.

'Valia Ammumma'. She was my grandmother's aunt and an authority on puranic stories. Kaali's story was my favourite. Bhavani Ammumma was such a raconteur. But she was so scared of the bloodthirstiness of Kaali that she would often scare herself after donning Kaali's character! At the end of her story session she would say 'Narayana, Narayana!' fervently and daub the special golden sandalwood paste she kept on her study table always.

Soon I filled Kaali in on all Bhavani Ammumma told me. I finished with how she loved Shiva and had renovated a Shiva temple recently.

'My child, who is Shiva?' She asked.

For the first time I wondered whether Kaali was being as perverse as the rest of the Gods.

'Don't play games with me Kaali!' I chided. 'As if I have to tell you who Shiva is!'

'I am Shiva', said Kaali. 'I am Shiva'.

Shiva

Shiva! Shivaa, rather. That was one of Her many names. Did She not respond to Her different names? After all, we differentiated ourselves with our names. But then Goddesses have different protocol. They have all the power too and it is very easy for them to change the rules as they go on.

It is stupid of people to believe that a man's true character comes out in adversity. He is struggling for his existence then and is generally on his best behaviour. He does not want to open up new fronts of conflict just then. He hunches his shoulders, tightens his stomach and gives a servile half smile with averted eyes.

Give a person lots and lots of money, power and the freedom to do what he wants to other people. Then his true nature seeps out. Whatever comes out will be true and that nature of his will burgeon till it hits a wall of resistance. It was always thus with the Gods too.

Despite my proximity to Kaali, I was sitting on the temple steps with Her, asking Her curious questions rather than composing verses praising Her

or asking Her for overwhelmingly predictable boons, that of salvation included.

I could sense the Goddess wait for my response. It was not the waiting of impatience, of need, of punctuation to further activity. She was waiting for me to catch up, in the meantime enjoying the thunderous snores of Kalidasa the elephant, whose tusks showed up more blue than white in that light.

'Why do you sit by my side and listen to me now? Why not go home and sleep? I could come to you in your dreams maybe!' She offered.

No way! I wanted to hear this only from Her fragrant lips.

'You love this, don't you? Likewise I love creation. There would be no more stories to say, to live if I did not create. Shiva is my creation just as I am His!'

'Why did you have to torture yourself to get Him? Lose Him once and then get Him back once again? Why not just marry Him....'

'...Goddess meets God. They fall in love and live happily ever after. Our stories would be so boring nobody would read them. Poets would be starved, so too book publishers, librarians. Besides when humans read how complicated love is for even the Gods, they may learn to be more generous with each other.'

Like every artiste, Kaali too was an incurably optimistic. They believed that music, poetry, painting, stories, dancing would all speak to the best of human beings and make them less fearful. Every conflict has its roots in some fear or the other. Every creation was harmony.

Entre Mahishaa

'Shall I tell you about the greatest love story ever created?' She asked me. 'It is also the most heart rending.'

I hated tragic love stories. 'Does it have a sad ending?' I asked Her.

'Love stories never end.'

For a long time Kaali sat silent and I let Her be.

'Have you heard of Mahishaa?'

As if on cue the moon vanished behind a cloud that I had not noticed. Which Devi bhakth would not have heard of Mahishaa? Mahishaasuramardini was one of Her longer names.

'His love affair was the greatest. Maybe Radha bhabhi had it with Krishna.'

I had heard of Mahishaa's cruelty, of his power, of his villainy. But love? Where was love connected with this demon?

Maybe his ambition was the result of a thwarted love. That happens to a lot of people. Love in other forms curdle and can become anything.

I stopped examining all the theories. Here I was sitting with the One who had lived through the episode, One who knew; maybe even the One who scripted out the whole story. I could not let go of my ego to surrender to Her version even! With a Goddess by my side, in such unique, beautiful circumstances I still had to cling on to my pride of knowing everything.

'Tell me Kaali', I said. 'And I believe you. However crazy it may sound.'

Kaali gave me a long look that felt like a soak in warm scented water.

Kaali started Her tale.

Mahishaa was born of great austerities and lust. His father was a demon who was a great practitioner of penances and his mother was bovine. After eons of celibacy, the father poured his seed into Mahishaa's mother who died in childbirth.

Caught between his maternal gentleness and paternal demoniac instincts, Mahishaa was confused. He had the head of a bull and the body of an adult man. But his DNA remembered enough of his sire's austerities. Mahishaa knew he was different and wanted to excel in his uniqueness.

Then Came The Gods

'In those days one got ahead through hard work. There were no shortcuts, recommendations, bribery', Kaali continued. 'Mahishaa decided to propitiate God'.

After checking out whether or not Mahishaa had staying power, God granted him his demands. Easily, guessably he wanted the best of all the worlds. He also needed immortality to enjoy those boons forever.

'Nobody is immortal.'

'Except you Kaali', I said for once not trying to show off but merely state a fact.

'Everyone who loves is immortal. The lover pining for his love, the woman whose very existence makes sense only when beheld in her lover's eyes, the terminal love of the moths for the flame, the serenading of frogs in the village pond, the growl-moan of mating tigers, the

spraying and scenting of dogs, the helplessness of elephants in musth, the teenager frantically 'whatsapp'ing, the late night SMSes, the chats… its all part of the process of love. The only question is who sustains it. That which is sustained is love. Those who sustain are immortal.'

My head was whirling. Almost every adult I knew was accusing their younger generation of degeneration and Kaali seemed appreciative of the communication gadgets most people shied away from! I tried to see if there was an I-phone tucked away snugly in the folds of Her garment.

Kaali laughed.

'We used the arrows of Kama, the breezes of springtime, lotus leaves to carry forward our love. They have changed their forms but the uses remain the same. Remember Energy….'

This time both of us laughed out. Waking at the unfamiliar sound, Kalidasan got to his feet and started feeding. I felt like him. There was a mound of fresh coconut fronds heaped by him and he was enjoying himself in the peaceful dark.

Inexplicably, my eyes welled up. Slowly I reached out and touched Her. Her skin felt like warm satin. She was nothing like what we had heard about, what we were told. Not even what we had imagined.

Yet in a strange way all that was part of Her!

And Story Time

'Tell me your story Kaali', I begged Her. 'From the beginning.'

Like all true lovers Kaali crooned out Her love story. Neither of us realised that She had changed Her mode of communication.

❋ UNIVERSE ❋

Who would dare fall in love with Shakthi
Ignore Her many weapons and woo Her?
Who would cast his eyes into Hers
A thrust he has no defense against?
Who would bare his chest and brace
For the three-pronged
Attack of Her spear?
Who would bellow in bovine bass AMBAY
When the whole worshipful universe
Hymned Her AMMAY?

❁ DEVI MAHAMAYA ❁

With 20/20 hindsight I can now see
That this could only have happened
This way
But not then Mahishaa!
How many years of penance do I do
For killing you, my black lover?

How can I forgive, how can I
Forgive myself for the wrong choice
The long, long life left for me to live out
As a great Goddess?
The whole Universe applauds
My battle courage.
All for those cowardly Gods
Who play games among themselves
And with their devotees,
With the casual cruelty of
The irresponsible.

I took the golden trident
I took aim
The thrust was mine
The choice was mine
The chest was yours
Your love was mine

Mahishaa! Your love was mine!
Yes your love was mine
To accept or then shred
And discard
Along with my sanity.

❁

And the pain came and when it did.

All I could do was to go quiet and sit.
Tell you to sit and write of our love
So unique, so crazy it sounded fictional.
He was the bull – bestial, beloved
And I the deified Goddess
Inaccessible, living on a snow mountain
Riding forth on a killer mount
Whose roar was enough to paralyse
If not kill
Cattle.
Cattle was Mahishaa's clan
Divinity mine.

How could I manage,
Tell me, how I can manage
This thing between him and me
That does not let me go?

❈ MAHISHAA ❈

Beloved, love
Come to me
Come to me.
Here I wait my head bent
Towards this earth that I rule
With the heavens above
And the hells below,
All of which I control.
My love, no hell was worse
Than this waiting for you
Woman Goddess.

Kill me then, consign me to death
If you will not have me
I who have decided for all
Leave this one decision to you
That will mean life or death to me.

❈ UNIVERSE ❈

What can they know, the wise ones
Of the pain of a Demon cursed to fall
Madly in love with a Goddess
Made just to kill him? How can they guess the
Devastation of a Goddess
Ordained to kill Her true lover,
Born as a Demon?
Born as the enemy of Her acolytes.

❈

Oh! They celebrated, how they celebrated
When your lover lay dead at your feet
Reddened by his blood
Which anointed the golden tips of your trident.
His roars died away.

Your ears hurt at the Sanskrit shlokaas
they hymned you with.
The flowers the Gods showered on you
burned your skin.
The golden throne they readied for you
looked like
An electric chair that had just electrocuted
your love
O! Goddess!

You gained quite a name for yourself
among the mewling Gods
Who wanted you to do their bidding.
They who forgot you once they secured
their kingdoms
They who abused their womenfolk that
you had made in your likeness.
Goddess you should have opted to accept
the love of the dead Mahishaa
Rather than the worship of a million men
and their attendant Gods.

❈

Mahishaasuramardini!
You would have been better off
Being uncreated by the Gods
Who got ideas way above their station
And forgot that you are the real creator.

Powerful, formless
Unlike the matlabi Gods
Who knew so well
When to use, abuse
Most of all when to
Stick labels on you
And dump you on
The head of that buffalo corpse
They called 'Demon'
Who, nevertheless, adored you.

❀ **MAHISHAA** ❀

I am your duritham.
My loving you and you condemned
To kill me
If you read anything
Apart from human hearts.
Would have recommended you read
Balzaac's story
'The Executioner'.
Does it not read, love,
Like your mini-autobiography?

❀

Lower and lower I bow my head
Louder and louder I low
In love, in rage
The more and more you stay away.

Balancing on your lion mount
Battle me, take me
Make me yours with a fatal flamboyance
That will defeat
The Gods gathering in the twilight.
Aspiring to something more than
Their limited selves,
They are clueless about!

❀

People say you are a Goddess Kaali
And that you will come in the form you
are called.
That's easy for me then love.
Hunger for you grew helplessly in me
With the frenzy kept only for demons.
You desired Shiva this way once long ago,
I am told.

A couple of kids and a few cycles of
creation later
Do you still retain that intensity for him?
Then you know what I am going through.
Come, deliberately to me now.
Shiva must have felt the same way
When the pull of your love lassoed him
To you, however unsuitable it was for an
ascetic.

Only completeness can make you a
Goddess
Not the superior position you take
Based on your far greater powers.
Let me engender in you this Shive
experience
Endanger, rather, in you this unsuitable
love
My darling turned Goddess.

My subjects whisper among themselves, in awe of you.
They say all the Gods chipped in to make you
They gave you their essences
But to me you are just a wholesome woman
One I desire with a helplessness that must be
The first death knell for me, if their gossip is true.

I should fight you and defeat you before anything you say
In a tone that seduces me as much as the sight of you
On your lion mount outside my gates.
I leave my kingdom behind,
For a second, I mourn my people who died for me
Killed by you.
I try to hate you and fail.
You try to make me fear you, my love
And fail equally spectacularly as I.

There is the scent of fresh blood in the air.
Your hair flies about like thick serpents
Lashing about in a frenzy of love-making all of its own
Your hair so black, so thick, so clean
I can smell the freshness of it.
I would love to oil your hair, running my hands through it
My fingers gently grazing your neck – a touch
Enough to quicken your breath though you face away from me.

I would love to wash your hair then
The water running off would be as fragrant
As a bower of wild flowers growing deep in the forest
Unseen by ordinary eyes.

I would dry your hair and wrap me in that dark glow
And inhale your smell.
I would just hold you my black beauty.
Yama gave you your hair, is it?
He is the God of Death I hear.

That's okay, wrapped in your hair shroud
I will happily await any death he has written for me
Because distance from you, my love
Means a kind of death even he,
Yama, can never conceive of.

MAHISHAA

❋

Why did it have to be this way?
I, a demon who loved you beyond all
And you a Goddess made to kill me.

I hear fountains tinkling in my palace
And imagine how you laugh,
My minions lay out silks for me to dress in
I desire nudity with you.
They hail me by my name and I strain
And listen to that silence that does not reverberate
With your whisper trying out my name
For the first time.
They touch my cloven feet reverentially
When I am ready to kiss your feet
Toe by iridescent toe.

Let your lion gorge on my bull mount
Or me, it is immaterial.
With myself in my animal body, in my demon mind
I have worshipped you on New Moon nights
Full Moon nights and time in between.
Do you want me to give up my kingdoms
My armies, my wealth I won from others
After such hard penance that one of the Gods themselves
Granted me all you see?
Do you want me to fall, fall again
Fail
Bleed
Hurt
Roar
Scream your name
With such agony
It is ecstasy of a different kind?
Do you want me to die, live again and
Die again
Live through lives as inconsequential
As the crown on my head?

I throw my last glance to the many loves
Stacked in my life as fetters
Keeping me away from you.
I smile once at him who warned me
Told me of your dangerous powers of attraction.
You could melt even the Ice God
With just a thought of yours.
Now take, take, take from me
All that I can give and beyond
Take it, it is your right, your due
From your demon lover
With whom your name shall be linked
Eternally
Rather than with any of the gods
Who claim you to be theirs!

❁ DEVI DURGA ❁

Bleed, bleed, bleed out
Your love for me, Mahishaa
Bleed out your life.

I am a Goddess
I expect no less from you, demon that you are.
Look at your buffalo face
The snorts that pass for words of love
The thump of your tail
Your cloven footfalls
Your erect penis,
A linga-prathishta all by itself
Die demon! Die!
Show me the extent of your love
Do you love me as your life?
Your breath?
Beyond your life?
Beyond all?

Go, then beyond all!
And you will see
Me
Wait
For you
There.

Will there be a time
When I am no longer a Goddess
Nor you the demon I must slay
To win accolades from flighty Gods
With quick-changing interests
Quicker changing passions.

Love was that which bound us together
Love was all that bound us together
Demon!
Die.
Lover!
Die
Love!
Die,
As I thrust my spear into your chest
That never had me nestle there
As my bestial pillow
I who rode a lion
And wore elephants as exotic earrings.

Yes, Mahishaa, it is indeed I
Who losing all but the fear of
What the Gods will say,
Understand your love
The loss of which I rue daily
Within my Goddess façade.

❋ MAHISHAA ❋

No love, I do not have to write only about you
My thoughts lead to you again and again
My pen just follows.

Who called you Goddess, nay deemed you one
When you were all woman?
Nothing about you is unfeminine.

Your thick black hair
Your eyes deep with an expression in them
That you do not let me fathom
The curve of your lips, your breasts, your ears
So soft like pink shells softened by the sea and the sunset
Your long fingers.

Your waist that I yearn to clasp
Your thighs I imagine on me as we sport
You on top of me always, love.
Your feet reddened, which guided your lion mount
With tenderness rather than force.

Your voice when you call out over the battlefield
'Mahishaa!'
Do I imagine or was there a wealth of love in it?
You who saw everything, understood everything
How could you miss the love contained in my misshapen body?
My love for you is as pure as a Himalayan stream
That comes dancing on boulders
Learning softness from them,
Day by day, dousing by dousing.

Let us pause in this war
The outcome of which is already decided.
All is fair in love and war, they say
Tell me love, which was it to be
What was it between us?
You sneaked a look at me, a weapon
That hit me fatally through all of my armour with ardour.

They tell me of a temple to you deep in the South
Where the poojaris are taught never to look at your face
But only at your feet
Lest your look scare them away so that they run

Leaving the Shrikovil doors open for anyone to enter.

Anyone who can withstand your deadly look, that is,
I know the ampere of your glance; it felled me.

As I said, I do not have to write only about you.
My thoughts lead to you again and again
My pen just follows.

Follow as I will your diktat
In this battle for supremacy
My love, my murderess, my beautiful one.

❋ KAALI DEVI ❋

Mahishaa, tonight is Ashtami night
My sleep seems over
As must the battle.

Both of us know it commenced
And ended
The moment our glances met in a fatal clasp
The conflict became one of another.
I fight my need to put my head
On your chest and cry
Tell you how much your love matters
The only thing of worth, in this creation.
Instead tomorrow I shall fight my lost battle
And your last.
Why link the cruel moon of Ashtami of both halves
With me,
To remind me I gave up absolute love
For the sake of a dubious power?

❁ UNIVERSE ❁

Fed on a primary diet of blood
Kaali
You don't realise the saltiness in your mouth.
Is that of your tears
As Mahishaa lay dead at your feet?
The look in his eye adoring
Even in death
That he gladly took from you.

❁ MAHISHAA ❁

Your look.
Your look was just all of love
Kaali.
So long as you look at me the way you do
Kaali
Come kill me
Again and again
Preceded by that look in your eye.
Not just love
Not just pain
Not just compassion
Not just passion
Just the way a woman looks at the one
She has to annihilate.
Yes, the one she knows, loves her.

❈ MAHAKAALI ❈

Lately Mahishaa, I feel something
Drain out of me
Much like the blood that will pour out of
The wound I am to give you.
Let us pause in this war and talk.

Both of us know how this fight will conclude.
You were made to love me
And I to lose you, worse destroy you
Knowing full well that no one will ever
Love me the way you do.
Mahishaa, do you know how much time is there
For a Goddess to live out
For an average era
In great Divinity?
After she kills her love
And for what the Gods may say.

Mahishaa, clear this one doubt of mine
You, who are so sure of your love for me.

❈ MAHISHAA ❈

Deck yourself out in your best, my love
It is only a question of time.

Others hear me as a roar
See me buffalo-faced and with a tumescence
Ready to ravish any female
Divine, bovine, human.
They need proximity to my power
They who never bothered to seek me
Find out if I AM at all!
Deck yourself out and sit
Singing by my gate
I shall come out by and by.
Your weapons glitter the way your jewelry do.
Raise your arm that looks too slender
To hold up the spear you will impale
On my chest
Your bangles jangle as a drumbeat to my heartbeat.
Ours was a pagan wedding, nevertheless, one of love
Our union was wrong, mismatched.

You a Goddess with no loins only mountainous breasts
On which the world feeds and feeds.
Gentle one you were made to kill
To destroy me.
Come, I am ready I wait.
All the drama I made was never to attack you
Or to defend me.
I did it so that others could extol your battle skills
Let them write shlokaas to you with my blood.
Your eyes defeated me long ago as I decided to enter this fight.

Just to gain you
For love is nothing but a battle
On a different plane.

❈

Your breasts they say
Smell of jasmine
Something that has not flavoured your milk!
Say those suckled by you
In wonder.
I know jasmine took on its fragrance
From your flesh, dear one,
Revealing your secrets to me
Like any lover does.

❋ UNIVERSE ❋

Black Goddess
Black moon hidden night
Black demon with
Black thoughts, black deeds
Black blood he spills
Black magic Goddess made
To kill the one who loves you
For the sake of the ones who use you.

●

Bull demon
Penance
Boon
Power
Ego.
Fear
Prayer
Creation
Goddess of
All Gods
Seduction
Bull Demon
Slave
Surrender
Love
Murder.

Woman
Alone
Incarnadined
In a Sea of blood.

❂ MAHISHAA ❂

You always chose duty
Over love.

Duty was admirable
But cold
Righteous
Holier than thou.
And love?
Love was tumultuous
Raging
Constant
Wound
Pain
Ultimately death
That is immortal.
Still I would choose
Love over duty
Time and again
My killer Goddess.

❈ UNIVERSE ❈

What will sustain him, love
Beloved
What will sustain him
What will make him rule?
A love of power?

Silly woman!
What are you but the power of love
Over reason
Fear
Conflict
Pain
Death
What are you red one, but love?

The flush on your face deepens
And becomes a fierce blush.
People will just look
At the red blood of the battle.
Your blood and his mingling in a way
Your bodies yearned for but never managed.
Demon and Goddess
With the whole of Creation
Packed in between like a wilting lettuce
Sandwiched between
Existence and LIFE.

❈ MAHISHAA ❈

It was hard my love to do penance
To the Gods who ultimately love flattery
Over ability, goodness even.
I earned all the power they gave me
Moment by torturous moment.
It was worth it.
What could I do that the devas were
Weaker than me
Had less staying power
Or was it that I fought better?
I grabbed all that I could, with the bloody right
Of a conqueror.
The Gods got together and tried a rebellion
I quashed with just a glance.
Sometimes I think power is right.
Look at the way the Gods quail before me
Look at the way I fail before your eyes
Urging me to a battle, the outcome of which
Was less fatal to me
Than to you, my love
In the end.

What did it matter that the lion roared
Staking out aural territory
Claws rending pieces of me
As an evil flavored succulent snack?
I just bullish to your
Goddessness?
Lovely one I desired as mine, my wife
To rule with me this uncertain universe.
What did it matter the spear carved with my name
Zooming in like a heat-seeking missile.
What did it matter the laughter of the devas
Those perfect forms concealing imperfections
Repugnant even to my bestial visage.
What did it matter the boon that undid me?
Tell me what did it matter finally, lovely one.
Death is ordained for all you know
You know it too beloved
You who bore the death of the greatest
Love in your life
With my going.

What did I want of you, except you
Woman Goddess
Enchantress
Beauty
My love
My dream so perfect it came at me
With death attached.
That attachment was fatal.

As I lie dying, bleeding by your feet
Wounded by your hands
Look into my eyes and read
Of your greatest love going away
But never leaving you.

❂ **UNIVERSE** ❂

Goddess, protector and huntress of souls
Do you seek your demon lover
That old bull
You brought down to his cloven feet
And his dying eyes clear of all accusation
Except that one of love?

❈ MAHISHAA ❈

Let me add up my sins as a lasso
To reach your blue misty distances
Where you skulk,
Peering down at your creations
Improving on your abysmal mess
Measuring themselves against you,
You eccentric artiste
Whose creations have taken over
A long time ago.

You watch the drama of life unfold
Its script long torn up
Left untranslated into human speech.
Let me consistently do wrong
To catch your attention.

How much the pious had to slave
To reach you finally!
The wicked who inveigled
You to slay them
Held you in their evil thrall
That you seemed to prefer
Over the prayerful calls of the devout.
I will destroy all that is considered good
And out of that debris you will rise
In complete splendour to annihilate me
And in that moment before my death
You shall look me in the eye,
Understand my silent call to you
To take up arms
Take me in your arms
Take me with your arms
Take me
Make me dead
Make me yours
Make me happy.

❋ **UNIVERSE** ❋

Between us there was only violence
They say you engender only violence.

Look at you!
Your blood wet tongue hanging out
Your roar that passed for laughter
Your dead bones jewelry
Shiva's violent inner conflict to resist you
Mahishaa's violent love for you
That culminated in his death.

Go further back
The violence of the big bang
That brought out this creation
From your desire.

The violent ripping away of this earth
Snatching soughing oceans as ointment
To cool its burning skin.
Yes violence becomes you,
Gentle mother of creation.

❋

What did you do with such alacrity
Lovely lady of both destruction and creation
At whose tender feet
The bull comes pawing its feet
Snorting and charging
And finally dying
As you held up the Universe lightly.

Yet another accouterment
In your trendy existence?

❁ MAHISHAA ❁

O love They call me demon
Abuse me, curse me
Wish death on me and
Rejoice as I lie
Dying
By your feet.
You were their Goddess
You are my love.

Let them celebrate, burst crackers
Gorge on food
Deck up your image
Only to drown it in the sea.
The paint they had daubed on you
Ran like my blood in different hues
And dirtied the ocean.

And I? I exult too
Quietly content to die by your hand
And lie, putting my dead head
By your tender feet.

❁

They saw only the demon in me
Never the love in me for you
They were happy to revile me
Call me bad names, attack me in groups
Spit on me.
I roared and they thought it was a threat.
I roared out my love for you.
They missed knowing me
For who I am, in the
Cacophony of their being.

And you, my love?
You go quiet
Eyes downcast or was it cast down?
You look at your own feet and see me
Supplicating, worshipping
For making you happy was my greatest desire
And possessing you a close second.

It is okay my love
Between us this silence
Broken by the hiss of the spear
The rip of my chest
A snort of your breath, or was it a sob
And then –
Eternity by your feet finally deigning to touch my dead head
Making it your footstool, my queen of Devas.

Stealthily Kaali
I whisper your name to me
Waiting for you to manifest out of the five elements
You created as building blocks
For this Universe.

Darling it was here that we met
Within this space and this time as the fabric
That held us.
One in which we embroidered our love story
The red threads of lust, the white ones of pain
And the black one of quiet joy in beholding you
Having you in me, bearing this love for you in me.

Dearest, will I have to drape this as a shroud for my love
Or will this be your attire as you come to me,
Your Mahishaa
Step by adroit step?

❈ KAALI ❈

I have left my hair unbound
Something unseemly for chaste wives
Women of high birth and of course
Goddesses
I leave my hair loose as I stand motionless.

Frenzied, the wind tries to be my hairdresser
Trying in vain for a demure look.
Thick coils of my hair wave in the air
Like so many serpents adept at yoga
They learned on the sly from Mahadeva.

No hairdo, ribbon or jewel fixes my hair
Its violence shows the turmoil in me
I refuse the crown the Gods extend me.

It is Death who gave me this hair
And I gave him death
He, that demon, who disturbed
The world order in one way
And me in a different deeper way.

Ganga could not have held on to my scalp
Though Her flow was always downwards
My head is reeling, my heart frozen
No, I shall leave my hair open, uncontrolled
Something that I never did with my love.

❈

Was there death ever for the Gods
Those puny entities who got immortality
For themselves as a double-edged sword
Cutting dead their illusions?

Only power counted, that ability to…
To make and bend laws
With Divine rights.
The Shlokaas extol love, the Vedas urge for peace
But tell me where would Ram have been
If he had just negotiated Sita back and left
Ravana in peace in his emerald kingdom.

Would Jesus be so revered, remembered
But for his death hug of the Cross?
I killed many demons with different
Power quotients, shapes, habits and boons
But it was only he who was linked to me
As if his was my first name and
What we did together, my surname.
Yes Mahishaa, by dying you defeated me
And immortalised your love way beyond Gods.

❈ LAKSHMI ❈

On Vijayadashami
The crowds gathered at dawn
Families with their children
Primed to start reading and writing
Their first script on rice
Their first words a prayer
Witnessed by the ghee lamp.

The priests were busy, very busy at
The feet of the decorated Goddess
Who had vanquished the buffalo demon
The night before
Standing now on the reddened sea of blood
That smelled like incense.

Only the illiterate girl child
Who had memorised the
Saundaryalahari
Saw tears in the Goddess' eyes as
She waited for yet another Navarathri
To come by.
Even fighting was a way of being together
With Mahishaa.

❈

Die for love, I thought.

I shall die for love
Following that demon before me
The one you had an
Unexplained relationship with
Something you never talk about
That something I gleaned
From the looks that passed between
The killer and the killed…
His dying for love
And your living despite love.

❋ MAHISHAA ❋

You are the repose in my sleep.
The satiation of my hunger
The rhythm of my music
The beauty of the moon
The warmth of the fire
The softness of love
The constancy of this battle
Between us, unequals though we may be
You are the life of my love.
You are what makes me, me
Yes, you are what unmakes me.

❋

So will you do my last rites love
Or will I gain veera-swargam
By dying in a battle
Especially one where you were my adversary?
Does your being my love
Lower my grade, deny me entry into Heaven
Where lesser warriors reside?

What should I expect this Aadi Amaavaasi, my love?
Having taken murder at your dainty hands
Shall I quit any expectations
Except the Eternity of my torturous Love?

❋

In the silence of the place that is
Neither creation nor annihilation
I know how much I loved you
How right that love was
How you deserved it more than
Anyone else I could think of.

I died for you because I could not live for me
You were my essentiality.
No one argues that breath is necessary
To sustain life
Why do they then wonder at my need for you?
Nothing mattered except your joy

In the silence of the place that is
Neither creation or annihilation
I wonder if you are truly happy
With your choice?
And I reincarnate each Navarathri
To give you more chances at the same options
Any of which I am ready to ratify
With my life, Mahishaasuramardini.

❈ KAALI ❈

Mahishaa you are forbidden for me.

My birth was just to kill you
It was something the Gods could not achieve
They gave me so many bribes to kill you.
You never did anything against me
We were strangers at best
Why should I kill you?
You were so reasonable
In a way the Gods are not.
They were scared of you – with good reason
Your power made them weak
They hated that
Their dealings were all based on power
And the ways to misuse it.

Yours with me, was just love, I know
Why else did you offer an undeserving Indra
His throne, just because I asked you to
Mahishaa!
If that was not love, what was it?
Flattery? A bribe for me?
But then I dare not accept
The greatest thing
Ever offered to me- that of your love.

❈ MAHISHAA ❈

Kaali! Stay!

This is just a line or two
To say how much I care
Don't worry
Always you will kill, and I die
You will have nothing to fear
From your Gods.
Whether you have to fear yourself
Is quite another matter!

❈

Kaali! After all that
You gave me death
In exchange for my love
You were the one giving.
I could only accept,
A courtesy you neglected
To give me.

❈

Everything about me was larger
Than anything else going around.
I was demoniac.
My ambition, the hard tapasya
I underwent to fulfill it
The boon I asked for
My greed ego power
All of which worked against the Gods.

My boredom at having nothing further
To conquer was removed
When I saw you
You happened my love
You happened to me
Did that work for the Gods
Or against me?
I am not sure
My hunger for you was in proportion
To all that was there in me
Were you ever truly angry with me
Or did you just kill me out of duty?
I died my love, at your hands
Yes Goddess
My love for you too had the same proportions
As life.

❈

My favourite colour is red now-a-days.
Red was after all the colour of blood
Fire was just a faded hue of my blood
With the equal heat of passion.

Kaali, why did you love blood so?
Lapping it up like a third rate vampire
Were you iron deficient?
Did it give you a longer tenure on earth each time round?
Did you need longevity?
Then why this obsession about blood, my love?
All you needed to do in our last battle
Was to sit on your lion mount
And just look at me
Your glance was enough to wound me fatally.

Fatality, was not my dying
It was my living without your love
A cruelty you spared me from, my love
My assassin,
I am grateful for your kindness.

❀

How I wait and wait and wait my love
For you to claim me in a battle
I had no chance ever of winning.
All was fair I heard in love and war.
Snaring me with your eyes
Snatching all from me
Without asking even
And then killing me
Was it love, was it war?
There is something crucial I have to ask
It is vital for my sanity
Did you kill me because the Gods wanted it?
Or did you kill me because you din't want me
To have the torture of a life without you?
One was because of callousness, the other concern
Both led to the same thing – my death.
People ask what is the point in any case?

For me all it means was, was it love, was it war
With you beautiful woman
With whom I was linked pre-birth, post-death.

The Gods knew that I would die
That too by your hands
I never knew.

It all started with my idle desire for you
A casual interest based on hearsay
When you decimated my people.
I was intrigued even within
My affront and my anger
When I saw you.
I hated myself for loving you
I wanted both you and the memory of you to die
To disappear, vanish from my life
To go! Run defeated to the Gods who made you
Just to fight me.
But then woman, Goddess, what do I call you
All that mattered to me was the look in your eye
The smile on your lips
If I could make you happy it was enough
Losing my life was quite okay
If that was good for you in any way…!

When I learned I was so powerful
That the mewling Gods crawled before me
Flattered me to my face
And conspired to assassinate me
Behind my back
As I put on the crown and sat on the throne
Gave generously to my favourites
Roared, behaved arrogantly
And generally was as obnoxious
As those who I had wrested power from.
Women crowded into my harem.
My throne had space for a female
I would deem queen of my heart
A vacancy that slipped furtively
Into my eyes and life and stayed
Until I met you
Singing on your lion mount
Like a village girl tending to her livestock.
Feeling your glance on me I learned
What power was, what it was not
For what is love, my love, except learning?

MAHISHAA

❀

When you crept into my soul
And then made it yours
What use do I have for this body
That comes with the Soul,
Something that Nature decreed?
Here destroy my body
You – who rejected my love
Without you by my side
Death has greater charms on me
Than that useless life, empty of vitality.

❀

If Life was just one set of molecules
Going about their job
Death was the same set of molecules
Constant, but for their work change.
See how dead cells push out hair
On a corpse
Blood congeals at the lowest part then
Black and static.
Stiffness and heaviness have taken over
Where breath was, before it fled
Leaving bodies as buffet spread for maggots.
Free of the spirit and its attendant baggage
Take me, make me yours and you, mine
Or kill me
Molecule shape shifter
It is all the same
Its all this set of molecules
Whether dead or alive.
Will carry your imprint
To fission, to fusion
Yes to fruition
My lovely woman of Life Sciences.

❁ KAALI ❁

I should have realised it Mahishaa.

I never did till now
That they all wanted me is true
But only for some purpose of theirs
The Gods, for destruction
And the people who petitioned
The collaborating Gods
To make me a Supreme Goddess
Wanted so many things from me
They composed the Sanskrit prayers
With those in their own mother tongues.

Only you Mahishaa,
Only you loved me for my own sake
It was your misfortune to do so.
And mine to know this and then
Do nothing about it.

❈ MAHISHAA ❈

My love they ask me to be humble
To pray with my head bent, eyes closed
As if I believed in Gods
Who claim themselves to be masters of the Universe
And all in it.
Were they such dumbos then
To create me as their enemy
That too one they could not defeat?
Were they such masochists?
And could they not understand
That once I met you my priorities
Changed drastically?
I could not be bothered with them anymore
Creating you as a joint venture
They did me a favour
They could have called in anytime.

Could they not begin to look at
That thing in me
Which everyone realises
But goes best without a name?
Could they not let us have a life together
Far from their heavens and kingdoms?
That I gift them as bride price
For you?

❈ KAALI ❈

Gods are nothing but mortalities
Of a different dimension, size
They too have their legends
Their story – span
Their time as the venerated
Worshipped
Their fortunes change as do
Their bhakthas.
Only love Mahishaa
Only love remains constant
In this unsteady world of
Whimsical Gods and more whimsical Fate.

❋ MAHISHA ❋

Soon Kaali, soon
Even my roars shall die away
Leaving you in a blessed silence
A numbness that filters out
The victory cry of the Gods
Celebrating my death.
For initial frenzied moments
They will extol you
Admit that you alone killed me
You alone could do it.

A few nights of revelry later
They will claim that it is indeed
They who made you
As a collective enterprise
You merely carried out
Their wish.

And that is when YOU will begin to wish
For me to be resurrected
Along with my love for you.

❋ KAALI ❋

You had nothing but yourself to give me
Which you did, flamboyantly
And I did not have even me
To hand over as a return gift.

I possessed only the darkness of the night
The silence of the deep Sea
The waiting of the mountain
The power of the bodiless wind
That controls and defines life
The lewdness of the Sun
That falls on all he sees
Like an ageing monarch
On a fresh young world.

Tell me how can I accept you?
Tell me how you can love me?
Whether woman or Goddess
I am equally doomed in my cruelty
To you, my demon, my lover.

❊ THE DEMONS ❊

It is always the lot of us demons to lose
And lose badly at that.

See the way we die, roaring awfully
Till it is over
See the way our red sinful blood
Flows over your feet
Like a wet primal kunkumaarchana
No priest officiated over.

No one seems bothered about our dead masses
Our corpses rotting in the angry glare
Of the Sun God
No one thinks of our funeral.
Which God or Godling would deign
Cremate us demons.
Garuda and birds of his ilk
Won't feast on our black scaly corpses
No natural scavenger exists in the plane
We were killed in.

Yes, only the bull-faced one among us
Escapes rotting, his carcass a footstool
For that lovely woman who killed him.

❋ **UNIVERSE** ❋

How come Kaali, that when you lunged
Into the Demon's chest
With a thick-poled spear, its tip
Split into three as it touched his skin?

Did Mahishaa's intense love
Break the edge into three
Or did it briefly stand
For those forbidden words
'I love you'?

❋

You are a Goddess who fulfills desires
Not a woman who can have ones of her own.
Why do you need love of THAT quality?
Don't you have devotees by the million?
Don't they satisfy you?

O Kaali do not look to the Gods who made you,
Nor the priests who claimed you as theirs
Hanging their arguments on a holy thread.
Do not look to the royalty who came to your temple
With more pomp than you were ever given.
Do not look to the devotees who
Worship you, no doubt but for things
They think you will get them.
THAT kind of love is extremely rare
But it exists in this world
Pledged to those lucky few…
Or were they unlucky?

Kaali look to that Demon who loved you
Who desired you the way you did
His caliber of love
Look to that Demon who loved you
And proved his love, by dying.

❂ MAHISHAA ❂

Maybe it was all for the best, love,
By dying I made my love immortal
And me to be a martyr for love.

Imagine our domesticity – we would be
Mismatched in all except our contempt
For the shallow denizens of the world
Both Divine and human.

Our children would be brilliant or total freaks
Like a German Shepherd-Daschund pup
Ill matched, ill mated.
Time, that lethal thief could have eroded
Our passion, leaving us to be a bickering couple
Or an indifferent one at worst.

Better that I died now and loved forever
Better that you yearned too, forever.

❂

Sometimes I envy Rakthabeejaasura.
He got you close enough
To lick up his blood, which made him
Ultimately die, it is true,
But he got proximity to you.
Did he feel all your licks even
When in embryo form
In every burgeoning drop of blood?
Did you feel him as a tiny grain
On your lapping tongue?

All I felt, my love, was your eyes on me
And this huge thing in me
That both of us know to be my love
For you.

❈ KAALI ❈

I know your love was pure, untainted.
All love is pure Mahishaa.
We are the fools who divide things into
Divine and demoniac
When all that matters is love
All that counts is love.

I cannot even be counted
Only worshipped
For my power is great enough
To annihilate you,
You who defeated the Gods roundly, openly
Yes, even me secretly, with your love.

❀ **MAHISHAA** ❀

A love like ours could only be fatal.

If it had to last forever, one of us had to die.
I chose the easier option of ceasing to exist.

You became a Goddess, their worship heaped on you
Like wreaths on the living, choking your breath.

That way my precious, our love will last
Steady in its tragedy.

❀

They called me demon
Was I then Ravana,
In some previous birth?
I wonder!
Handsome and with ten heads
When I see my face reflected
On your ten toes
As I cuddle up to your feet.

❀

There was a time in my life
When you never existed.

Without you I was quite okay.
Unwittingly incomplete maybe
But quite fulfilled.
Not knowing you
I never missed you.

I fought, ran my kingdom
Drank and whored around
Things which leaders do
To make themselves believe
That they are happy
And that it was really worth
The bloodshed, the pain
And the fatal destruction of time.

Having seen you once in the dawn light
With a fragrant wind wafting from you
That made your carnivore mount
Smell like shy bowers that scent the night
Nothing matters except proximity to you.

MAHISHAA

Close enough that I can see the joy in your breaths
Sense, rather than see the happiness in your eyes
As they caress my face, your fingers following.

Mahishaa the king died then.

And was reborn as Mahishaa your slave
You condemn me to death
I have no complaint
These are but ordinary events in a life
Pledged sans conditions to you.

❈ KAALI ❈

Mahishaa, worship was pleasing to me
I confess as I tally what my devotees
Do to me, for me
And what I give them in exchange.
I enjoyed the praise they propitiated me
with.
I liked my Goddess status conferred on me
By needy Gods and humans alike.
But nothing made me more woman,
Pure Shakthi
Than that love in you
For me.

❈

In those lonely nights after I killed you
I realised my two greatest losses
Was the time I wasted to come to you
And the love I opted to discard
For deification by others.

❈

In Life all that matters is love.
Death being only the runner up
For primacy of position.

Why do I sense your grinning to yourself
As if I had tallied and talked nonsense?

Demon, I am a Goddess! Remember!
Not some cheap woman you could hire
From the temple grounds
Sitting guard over devotees' footwear,
My eyes at their loin level.

Now if only I were that Mahishaa
I would gladly be hired for love
The way the priests assure people

That I can be hired to do their bidding
With elaborate poojas with appropriate
Dakshinas, which satisfy only them.

❋ THE GODS ❋

What a loser!
I could hear the collective opinion of the world
First he betrays his dad's piety, his uncle's too
And his mother's gentleness.

He goes through pure hell
But gets so much power, there is
None like him in the Universe that we know
Nor have heard of an equal
Major Gods shun him in fear
The minor ones are in his employee
The entire creation bows to his will.

And then he throws it all away
For – can you believe it – love!!!
Has he gone mad?
Has power gone to his head so much
There is no space for good sense?

Who does he think he is?
Has he looked at a mirror ever?
He is a demon, an ugly one at that
Bestial!
Would She look at him, let alone
Love him?
She would be MUCH better off as a celibate for life!
We knew she would refuse his love
But the idiot, the prime idiot
To give up his power and all he made
For her sake!

Love sounds so good
Alluring
But we Gods know it does not exist
We did not manufacture it
It was not expedient to do so.
We are comfortable with worship
It is dignified and maintains protocol
Where we Gods, our attendant priests
And our devotees have fixed places.

But, love?
Ah! That was wild
Like the rush of flood waters
During annihilation
Or the tenderness of OMKAR
Before creation
Both of which we never could control.

He pursued her for love
And she killed him
Her response was apt.
It would destroy us

MAHISHAA

If love really existed even as a fugitive.

Love would teach joy and together
They would breed truths
Which are anathema to our very survival.

The world needs Gods
Not truth and love.

She got it right!
After all, many bits of us went into
Her making
Her genetic disposition is quite okay.
No, no

Don't think we use the Goddess
She just helps us
We are of her caste so its fine really.

What!
Did we REALLY hear the dead demon
Tell her to use his head as a footstool?
Did she agree – my God!
What a ridiculous perch!
She should'nt even touch his corpse.

…She refuses to move…
And even calls herself
Mahishaasuramardini.

✼ MAHISHAA ✼

You were violent always.
Your violence was love.

You caught the Ice God by the throat
As He swallowed poison, thinking it
Was just an emanation from the snakes
He wore as jewelry.
You saved His life.

You ARE His life!

The Gods muttered,
'Look at her audacity
How dare she be so forward and
Strangle her husband?
While we watched
That image etched in our divine eyes
That Ice God gave you a tender look
And went back to His tapasya.'

I knew the love in your gesture.
Why don't you put your hands around
My neck, even to squeeze out my pranaa,
My pranaa!
I am amenable to all, love,
That entails your touch
Yes, even if it is to kill me.

❂ KAALI ❂

Tell me Mahishaa,
What do I do
In this world
Where it is okay
To kill a stranger
But not to love him?

✺ MAHISHAA ✺

I was a yummy snack
For your lion mount; as was my bull vehicle
Designed so that I could alternate easily
Between being the rider and the ridden
To confuse those who desired
My destruction
As their birth right.

Did I ever beg you to stop the carnage?
Half dead fighting you, did I negotiate
Did I compromise?
You were the agent of the Gods, it was clear
You are my love,
You were so from the moment we met
Let me lose my power, my kingdom, my life
It's a bargain for me
Death at your lovely hands is salvation for me.

❋ UNIVERSE ❋

Will it not start to pall
The oft-repeated story
Of the inappropriate love
Between the demon and the Goddess
Both used to power, but new to love?

Better learn hymns by rote
Empty of emotion.
Better give new dhothis to the priests
Topped with crisp new notes
Of the highest denomination
Weighed down with gold coloured coins.
Better feed the Brahmins
Who have made a career of eating
For the sake of dead ancestors
And living hopes.

Who cares for love?
Not even that Goddess
Who chose worship over love....

❋ LAKSHMI ❋

Love sounds so good, one can talk of it
Drunk, sober or on the podium
During maudlin evenings
When school friends living in other cities
Visit for a night without family.
It sounds so noble to give up all
For the sake of love, be it for romance
The solid feeling of friendship
The distant love for the country
Flavoured with violence and legends.

But then love is never giving up
Never sacrificing.

Love is celebrating the best in you
With the ease of a fait accompli.
Love is that dangerous happiness
That assassinates the mundane.
Love was the only link
Between the buffalo demon and that lady
Who appropriated his life
In exchange for his love.

❊ **UNIVERSE** ❊

They say we need the night for the day
Pain for joy, silence for sound
Light for dark and the metaphysical
Good for evil.

Opposites not only attract
They sustain.
Ask the demon who loved
And the Goddess who killed
Ask them what existence
Both of them can aspire for
Without each other?

❁ MAHISHAA ❁

You tore my heart out from me
Impaled it still beating, on your spear
Yet I had no fear
No regrets for throwing my
Boon-awarded life away
For just a chance of winning you.

Did you want to implore me to desist?
To stop?
To end all my desires and then
Maybe end up meditating by your side?
You who desired the good of this world
That I so casually overturned.

There's my blood on you
Yours on me
Your eyes glow with induced rage
Or was it a film of tears
You dared not shed for me beloved.

Your lion steps on my corpse, on my blood
And walks away
His red footprints matching
Your vermilion ones, carrying you
Far, far away
But I riding pillion, as your memory.

❋ UNIVERSE ❋

The Gods who made Kaali dumped her
Once their use of her was over.
Human beings evaluated her capability
And petitioned her to do their work as well
For after all were they not too like Gods
But with less luck not to be thought Divine?
Only Mahishaa the demon she slayed
Curled up by her feet, adoring her.

❁ LAKSHMI ❁

They claim they love poetry, stories
And that they let their children grow up
To be different from them, but happy.
They exhort you to follow your heart.

Do not believe them.
There is no money in poetry.
Stories are useless unless made into
Big budget movies that deviate from the book.
Children are fed, clothed, schooled
Just to become clones of clones.

From following your heart – Desist!
Ask around what happened to that old
bull demon
With the good taste or temerity to fall in
Love
With a Goddess, no less.
His heart over powered his self
Led him to his death, his life long hypothecated
To his love.

❈ UNIVERSE ❈

Kaali with her drunken rolling eyes
Fangs, nails and skull necklace
Was fearsome.

She inspires terror
People worship her to avoid her anger
You can't even look at her
Without quailing.

But her Mahishaa
Loved her the way she was
Way above her wise Saraswathi self
And vivacious Lakshmi self.

Lakshmi

'Well, tell me now who loved me the most. You know the whole story now', said Kaali.

'Mahishaa.' I was sure. 'Undoubtedly!'

I could feel a quiet, intense joy radiate out of Kaali. There was a sense of relief too. She knew that I COMPLETELY believed Her story, preposterous though it may have sounded to some.

Was our nocturnal chat a welcome break for Kaali? People always found it harder to believe nice things. Certain people would have deemed Kaali mad. Her intensity and demeanour was truly frightening, till you looked into Her eyes, at which point you could easily see what a softy She was!

She believed in Love. She had lived Her life on the tenets of love. If there was going to be any chance for this world to survive, it would be only through Love.

A sudden idea struck me. What if I was able to prove the reality of the legend of Mahishaasuramardini NOW?

Human beings were those who believed in conflict, far too easily. They did not believe much in Love. Lust, maybe. But the idea of a deep and enduring love sounded outlandish to them. But then, Love was always in the air. She was there. All that was lacking there was a Mahishaasura! We were living in an age which desperately needed not only Love, but a belief in it.

'Kaali, I shall desire you like Mahishaa did. And you do to me what you did to him', I suggested. I was game for such an incident. 'We will then show human beings what the essence of Life is!'

There was a deep silence.

'Oh love, do you realise what you are talking about?' whispered Kaali almost to Herself. But I heard Her. I quite liked the fact that She had called me 'love', that too in that tone.

Yes, I knew that I was forfeiting my life to attain Her. It was okay. The deal was a bargain for me.

Quickly we hatched out a plan. The whole epic had to be remarketed if anyone was to believe in so great a love. She was there after all. Filling me, She would make me capable of a Mahishaa-proportioned love for Her.

Kaali checked my willingness for this scheme over and over again. Had I asked Her for moksham She would have had to consider giving it seriously. Refusing me would have been leading me up the spiritual garden path, only to bang the gates of heaven into my eyes and that would have certainly been in bad form.

Kaali felt that I was going overboard to validate Her story. She was delighted and guilty in equal parts! But then She knew that human beings trusted their own tribe over Gods all the time. Just look at the Godmen and women and the burgeoning cruelty done in the name of Gods, ordered by other human beings! All that just showed the superiority of human beings to themselves, over anything Divine.

We had a lot of planning to do. The incident had to be like a perfectly executed play. At the end, the audience would be called upon to give a verdict based on what they had just witnessed. They would have to introspect. Would they believe in love?

It sounded like a naïve plot, a 'and they lived happily ever after', fairy story. We also knew that the truth was often very simple. It became complex only when someone tried to manipulate it to market it for mass consumption, ignoring the fact that for each person there was a distinct truth that he or she had to arrive at.

She was there as the Goddess and I as the Demon who loved her. I desired Her. It was much easier to lust after such a beautiful Goddess rather than learn reams of Sanskrit (a language that very few people conversed in) in Her praise. What started out as an intriguing interest grew to lust and then enduring love.

Sitting on the steps still, Kaali discussed all the possibilities. Kaali wanted the venue to be an apt one. The timing had to be perfect; so too the action which had to run smoothly from the beginning to the end. Kaali and I decided to settle on the venue first. There were so many places of worship to choose from. It was not to be a very crowded one. Many things could go easily unnoticed amid the clamour and bustle of those places. Nor could it be a totally isolated, remote temple where there would be no witnesses but sleepy poojaris and the Goddess Herself!

Suddenly, Kaali struck upon an idea. We were, after all, going to bring alive one of the most vibrant and ancient incidents in the narrative of the Goddess. Kaali knew just the perfect place for this.

In the very middle of the city, there was an old, dilapidated temple, with wooden doors which were supposed to have the strength of iron. A *Kaali Bhagavathi*, supposedly the one after Her killing the demon Mahishaasura, was said to be in this shrine.

Old timers had heard stories from their great grandparents that this Kaali was the one who protected the town. No outsider with hostile intentions could stay near this town even for more than three nights. They were all scared away by dreadful roars of a lion at night. This was audible only to them.

Commerce in the city was excellent as was the fertility of the land and plentifully available potable water. The outsiders soon realised that so long as this Kaali was pleased with the people of this land, they would be unconquered. In a ploy to reduce the power of this magnificent Devi, forty- two families got together and threw cloth saturated with menstrual blood into the sanctum-sanctorum. Simultaneously, they dug up the statue of the demon Mahishaa looking up adoringly at the Goddess' face and took it away from the sanctum sanctorum.

The Kaali there was a Mahishaasuramardini, or slayer of the demon, Mahishaa, who then became incomplete and, therefore, diminished in power. Henceforth, bad times started for the land and the temple that guarded it.

The forty-two families and their henchmen had all met with horrible deaths. Some of the prime movers of this group were left BEGGING for death, as their very existence was awful. They found it hard to get people to look after them, despite their enormous wealth. The stink which arose from their decaying, rotting bodies were untenable even for their neighbours.

Terrified, some of their kinsmen built a huge Lakshmi Narayana temple abutting the old Kaali shrine. Shri Narayana was reclining on the thousand-hooded Serpent, Shri Anantha. Along with His consorts Bhoomi Devi, Mother Earth and Lakshmi Devi, Goddess of Wealth and the elusive Nila Devi, the whole Universe was depicted there, adoring Shri Narayana, also called Shri Pallikondeshwarar.

The keen displeasure of the ancient Kaali seemed to have become slightly blunted. It was then that the largely-ignorant population decided that they were going to build a magnificent Shri Mahalakshmi shrine. After all, She was the Goddess of Wealth and with money anything was possible!

The fear of the population, the ignorance of the priests who were fast forgetting all that they had to learn, practice and sustain, as against their mere birth into families and the mindless movement of the masses, pushed for the primacy of money above Divinity.

Much time had elapsed since then. Worship at the Shri Mahalakshmi shrine had also become routine. It would seem that everyone was forgetting that propitiating Deities was anything but mundane!

For some reason, this Kaali had been all but forgotten. Now the Goddess was making Her ire felt sans pooja and, of course, sans a proper sanctum sanctorum within the temple premises. There was a dire need to propitiate Her. I would do so. My love was the bait and when She did deign to appear for love, things would be set aright once again.

People would see the subtle interplay of love, power, conflict and resolution. How easily contemporary people had branded Mahishaasura as a villain, someone who richly deserved the annihilation meted out by the Goddess! He was pure evil for them. Kaali was going to teach them the truth!

❀ **UNIVERSE** ❀

What is love?
Ask Mahishaa
He knows well
The fixity of it.

See it
In his dead eyes
Still adoring Her
Who killed him
And uses his head
As a step up
To Her Divinity!

❈ MAHISHAA ❈

Tell me darling black love of mine
I see myself expanded ten times
Like a genetically modified Ravana
As I lie by your feet
Was it my bloated ego
Highlighted thus?
Or my love for you
You could only acknowledge
By my reflection on your toenails?

❀ KAALI ❀

Shiva meditated on Vishnu
Vishnu did pooja to Shiva.

The whole World worshipped me.

Me, Shakthi no one could do without
Did anyone bother
To ask me if I was lonely?
Whether I missed others' company
Just once in a while?
Let no one notice now
My eyes sliding on and away
From Mahishaa
Who I know loves me!

❋ LAKSHMI ❋

When I write in black ink,
It comes true, after all it is
The colour of your skin
That which I see when I lie dead
With my optic nerve
Losing all electrical impulses
From my brain.

They light a row of wicks around me
In coconut halves
The thick smoke from them
Makes my corpse look as if
I am still breathing.
Though I am strangely inert!
People look to see if my chest
Rises and falls in rhythm.
My fat tummy too,
Though strangely flattened
Though my dead weight seems
To have gone up!

Did the spirit I carried in me
Hold up so much?
Maybe I lay dead thus, Kaali
After you had taken away
The best in me, which was just you!

❈ MAHISHAA ❈

Yes my darling, it was foolish of me
To fall fully in love with you
Sight unseen even; I had heard your song
Your fragrance came wafting
Down with the breeze
Before gossip about you
From my excited subjects.
Now bit by bit, hack off bits of me.

What need I mine eyes anymore?
They have done their job
They have seen you.
My voice, let it grow rusty
Disused, as you refuse to hear
My words of love.
My nose has inhaled your scent
From far and near
All other smells are not for me.
My ears strain to hear your whispers
Albeit they are orders to your lion mount
To claw me deeper.

My skin yearns to feel you next to it.
Castrate me, I have no further use
For loins, henceforth, celibate
By your rejection
Kill me, deadly assassin,
Deadlier love
By dying I shall love you, forever.

❈ LAKSHMI ❈

Till they cremate me, they will fast.

Sweetened black tea being offered
To all who visit and all who stay
Looking helplessly at the inert me
They will sit quietly
They have cried themselves dry.

The wailing will start again
When they lift me up for the pyre
They cannot bear to think
Of my short hair as gone. Whoosh!
My skin will heat, split, crackle
Then collapse on my boiling oily flesh
The adipose tissue will make
The fire burn brighter
Like oblations of ghee on a Homam.

The smell from there will be sickly sweet
Burning on a non-edible Tandoor.
I would have liked to taste a fillet of me
Garnished with lime and chilli powder
Which would have melted in my mouth!
Like a painfully carved out
Cordon bleu dish!

Meanwhile I shall lie quiet
My gaze on that space
Between my eyeballs and eyelids
Where She stands
Erect, with a half-smile on Her lips.
Obviously, She too has waited
For quite some time, for this.

Something She lets me realise
Only when my closed eyelids
Have shuttered in Her place.
Now I smile my half smile
Of repose and recognition.

People there, shake their head and say
Did you notice how peaceful she looks?
With you my darling,
I can have only Bliss!

❂ KAALI ❂

Replete in your love
Why do I still look for approval
From the Gods who think
They created me?
Your stand is very clear
You love me
Woman that I am
Whom they want to make
Their own Goddess.

❈ MAHISHAA ❈

Cows were venerated, pampered
By that Krishna, he I would have loved
To have as my brother-in-law
Being kin to you, my darling.

He, had he been around,
Would not have alienated me
Calling me bull-headed.

I think he alone would
Have understood
Forbidden Love
That bloomed unbidden in me
Like cancer cells,
Finally destroying the whole body.

❈

Wounds bloom on my chest and neck.
That pain was nothing compared
To your rejection of me
And my love for you.

Demons are inferior beings
Their love equally low class
But still it is I
And it is you I want.

❈

Darling you came bearing in your hands
That weapon with which you kill me
To pierce me through.

The illustrators had a field day
They painted my being killed
With a spear through my heart
Mauled to death by your lion mount
Decapitated by a discus, sword even
Your cohorts hacked at me
From the back
Still I stood head bent, accepting.

Whatever came from you
Was just a gift for me
For it had come from YOUR hands.

❈

So, the Black was obviously you.
The White your Shiva
With whom you had
A special relationship.

The red, my blood I let you spill.

MAHISHAA

The brown Earth drinking it
To birth green shoots rising
The yellow flowers dancing
Orange butterflies flitting
The blue sky looking down
Witnessing silently
That all colours are you, my love and
Without you, drabness colourless
This vibrant Creation.

❀

Let's not talk about love
My black lover
Let us not talk politics
Philosophy, conflict.

Let us talk of the Moon
Rising in the sky
Hiding her rotundity
With tucked-in cloud fabric
Which the randy stars rent
With their sharp corners and angles.

Let us then wonder why
We look at the Moon
And let its silver soothe us
From the dark velvet of the sky.

My darling after all, it is to you my love
And for you that I lost
My kingdom, my heart
And most easily, fortuitously
My body.

By taking away my life, love,
You took away my pain.
There was a hidden kindness
In your vaunted cruelty to me, dearest.

They took one look at you
And named you the winner.
I was that demon who was
Tasteless enough to bear
A bull visage
Who had the temerity to woo a Goddess.

Knowing you to be
My assassin-in-waiting
They compute my life
And judge me a flop
A failure, all the more as I had
Won it and lost it all
For the sake of a woman like you.
Yet and yet, when I compute,
Look at you who I have loved
I see, to my maybe-prejudiced eyes
Only Perfection.

I will concede
Agree that enough love is
When love exceeds life.

Will you then agree
That for me to agree
To be killed by you
Was enough love
For you, in me?

❋ **KAALI** ❋

Mahishaa, why was love
Not enough?

Love for power
Love for making your lover happy
Being greater than the former.
I no longer know
What love is.
What power is.
I only see your warrior face
With pleading eyes
Yes Mahishaa, I need to know no further.

❋

Yes I was regal enough
To demand and get a footstool
Worthy of my feet
The severed head of that bull demon
Was the greatest.

Yes, I was woman enough
To realise I fought me
More than I fought him
And whatever the World may say
He won.

❂ **MAHISHAA** ❂

The sharpest weapon I felt
Was your rejection of my love
The softest one
The thrust of your armaments
Ending this life of mine
In which you refused
To be my queen.

❂

Just playing for time, I recount
My past battles, all victorious.
You are not interested, I can see.

You ARE victory
Why should you be bothered about
Tales of valour
Won battles, lost causes.
I see the expressions
Fleeting across your face
As I talk.
No. Love did not make an appearance
With a quicker disappearance.
I enjoy looking at you
That is all I want when I talk to you
Brave, brilliant warrior that I was
Losing my heart decisively, to you.

❂

The battle sounds were always there
Whenever we spoke my love.

Conflict was there between us.

I thought love was the best, not war
But I guess that's true only
When we discuss philosophy
Not actually live it.

It was ALWAYS me and mine
And our group
Not us – you and me – and a group
We could have made.

They brand me demon, evil
Who created me then?
The anti-God?

While God created the Devas
You were a thought.
To be a process of Creation
They thought they all made you
Giving gifts of and from themselves
But you embody the BEST in all.
What do they know, they
Who are full of themselves

MAHISHAA

That love took one look and
Being fleet of movement – left.

But then I, doomed to be in love
With my assassin – see you
The way you actually are.

❀

The ones I sought out were a few.
Many sought me out
Whether out of lust or ego
Or simple avarice, I do not know.
It feels good to bed an Emperor
Some hope to get pregnant
With my bovine seed, give me an heir
I could leave my kingdom to
Something that interested me the least.

I am through with the motions of love
Or stale desire masquerading
As genuine attraction.
I am as much a Yogin, an ascetic
As I was a sensualist.

I took over kingdoms
Because battles were interesting
They held my attention
For a short while at least.
Until I saw you.

All in me melted and
Congealed to a goo
You can shape the way you will.

You seek my surrender
You can; you have rendered
This proud warrior of many battles, me
To be nothing but your ardent lover.

❀

Your Sunabha worked
Like a boomerang
It scythed my head away
And bore it to your feet
Where it belongs
And you are in me
Where you belong.

❀

Yes darling, I was wounded
By the bite and the maul of
Your lion mount.

The hissing slice of your Sunabha
Cleanly chopping my head
Dropping it by your feet.

Most of all your ability

To say 'No!' to my love for you
I timorously tried to hand over to you.

❁

The crackle of my pyre
Turns into the silent cackle of my skull
Which was covered for years
By my skin, flesh and accessories
And the stories that I learnt to speak out.

No one thought of my skull
Not even I.
The poojari's well-placed jab
Cracks it in the fire.

Did my spirit escape through my cranium
As is the optimal path for Salvation?
Life grows out of the umbilicus
I know.

Where does Death exit from?
All I know is the inconveniences
Of my body.

With a few 'Kaali' words stuck on
Like sequins in the twirling skirts
Of the beggar girls....

❁

Strange that in our battle
My hooves gouged out the Earth
And that read as 'Love'.

My horns ripped the firmament
The scattered clouds read as 'Love'.

My tail slapped out tsunamis from the Sea
The foam read as 'Love'.

But you my darling
You failed to read the love in my eyes.

❁

I figure out only now why the Gods
Created human beings.

The Gods control, the Demons lust
Only these stick figures in a round world
Know to love – its bliss its pain
And most of all hope
That thing which never dies
That thing that never left my dying gaze
Looking upon you with Love.

❀

At the point of death I seek for
The truth deep in your eyes
Far beyond the fatal thrust
Of your spear.
That death lunge soothed me.

It quietened the pain of your refusal.

My heart was full of you
Did you wound yourself then
Or did you too hurt in a way
Far worse than mine
Doomed to be born to kill your lover
Doomed to know the exact extent
Of his love for you
Doomed to be worshipped, venerated
But loved? I doubt it.

Your compatriots, the Devas, know
Flattery and transactional relationships
But then again, love? I do not know!
I look in me and find you
I look outside and find you.

My body was the sole obstacle
For you to mingle with the you in me.

Bliss to die by you, remove my body
Consign it into flames
Which burn like the Love
I bear for you.

❀

Just leave us be! She and I.
I will vacate your celestial throne
And kingdom and go away with her.

I will sit by a cool brook and dangle
My cloven feet in the water
And talk to her of so many things
Which are so important to lovers.
It's okay if she doesn't love me.

It's okay if she rejects
My outpourings of love
I will still get to see her
The curve of her cheek, her left breast.
Hear the music of her anklets, bangles
Catch the heady fragrance off her
Watch the wind play with her hair
The way I yearn to!
We will just be two beings in Creation
Not connected, yet not disconnected.

This will be the only Life I ask for me.
Kingdoms bore me, as do armies
I have seen too much blood flow

For no real purpose
Maybe there is no purpose
In this love too
But it will make me happy
And THAT is purpose enough for me.

❁

Darling, a tiny fragrant white flower
Fell from your hair as you walked by.

You did not know it.
There is enough of the bovine in me
To chomp it up as a snack
But no!
Gently I pick it up and inhale
Your fragrance far sweeter
Than this lucky flower's
Yes, this one which touched you
Before falling.

❁

Kaali why do I return to you
Again and again
As if I can never really
Get to leave you?

There are apsaras more comely
Demonnesses, humans even

With the added advantage
Of their having loved me
Desired me, to say the least
For my vast powers
The godlings as my servants
My genitals
My legendary skill at lovemaking
My blood red eyes
My animal scent
My voice that was like
Gravel wrapped in velvet
My night sky skin
Draped taut over a physique
The War-gods could only slaver at!

Then just why my black love
My fatal attraction
My final celebration
Why would I throw it all away
For a mere smile from you?

❁

For me love has a shape – it is you
Death has a shape – it is love
Darling, all the fight has gone out of me
Now I desire what YOU desire.

You will not let me love you
Even if you could swing it

Past the Devas.
I take the tsunami building in me
To be a tiny splash
In a children's pool.
I have withheld my love
It makes the blood from my wounds
Replete with unrequited love
For you
I would like it to end quickly.
Only my body takes my side
And loosens its grip on me.

I shall leave my corpse as your trophy
Your victory stand, that you can
Clamber on to
Holding my horns for balance.
To desire you was a sin, remember?
I have paid my Karmic dues
Does Karma not affect the Divine Ones?

❀

Yes, you were worth it all.

It was YOU that I was
Going to possess
You, who possessed me effortlessly
Brazenly almost.
You made a fool of me
To my subjects

They were used to seeing me
Always in command
Now I am like a teenager in love
Formless in my surrender to you.
The Gods who made you
Laugh derisively.
Where was the mighty Bull Demon
Who ruled the Earth
The kingdom of the Devas
The very Universe as they know it.

Here was I Emperor of all my
Desired domains,
Curling up, lying, dying
By your tender feet.

❀

And He spoke of us
Saying you had to be drunk
To kill me.
Dutch courage at it's best in dulcet
Sanskrit.
Yes, they can hymn you, worship you
In any which way they want.
But He too saw your, your naked soul
The way I did.
But then I saw
Your naked refusal to look at me even
For a single glance

MAHISHAA

That would have convinced you
To throw away your armaments
Here and there
And run into my arms
Our love would have made our world.

Now I lie dead and you bear my name
As a prefix
That identifies you as my killer
And yes me, as your obsessed lover!

❀

How many times have I used
Urgent phrases
Rough words to convince you
Of my love for you?

Sometimes I imagine
Your slow smile
A soft blush on your cheeks
As you lower your eyes
Maybe scared to let me see
The depths in you
That you have started plumbing lately.
I imagine your voice
As you call me 'Mahishaa'.

The 'asura' was a suffix
Given to me by the Devas.
I imagine your petal soft hand
In my paw
You, mirrored in my glittering eyes
I love you
I need you
I want you.
Of course my body aches for yours
But, lust, my darling
Was just biology with you.

I yearn to feel your hands
Threading through the
Rough pelt of my head
My inhaling the breath
You exhale on to me.
I desire to touch the
Rounded calf of your feet
Your fingertips
I want to count the lines on your lips.

I dare not seek to go
Beyond the silk drapery on your chest
One that conceals your heart
Maybe with a drop of kindness
For me, a soft corner
For my colossal love
If not actual reciprocation
Dark love of mine!
What have you done to this poor animal
So so so much in love
With you?

So that was the story of my life.

For you, I may have been
A foe of your friends
Expendable, killable.
What was the use of my being around?
The Devas hated me
They were terrified of my strength
They were jealous that I wanted
Time with you – and your love in return.

The throne of Heaven was
Just a convenient seat for me.
Yes, I was used to Power
I had the right to wield it the way
I wished
No obliging Goddess came along
To help me, I had to fight alone.
It is okay
I was successful in many ways
You could call me a flop in another way.
But I have loved you dearest
In a way that makes
These very Gods look miserly.

❋ PASSION ❋

I could freely lust
Even after the wives of the Gods
But love was forbidden for me.

She too could only meet up with me
In the guise of battle
One, which had already decided
My fate in my words of love
Written out in my blood.

Let it then end soon
My undying love for her
And her terrible choice
All held in the salt grip
Of an ocean of unsaid love.

Proximity to you
Intoxicated me.
There were three prongs
On your Thrishul
Full of need for you
I pulled it to me
Thinking it to be
Your soft five fingered palm.
Somewhere my cohorts
Yelled, 'She's wounded him!'

Yes, she wounded me long ago
With her glance
Wounds bloom on my chest
With the deep red of Japakusumams
So dear to you
This is enough of a wedding garland
For me.

❈ SALVATION ❈

Darling, what long words you use
To describe simple acts
Of my merging in you
Like the mountain born rivers
Into the waiting Sea.

Patrolling the beach, incessantly
What ideas you think up
For this melting of me into you
Lovers, whose love
Transcended bodies into rare realms
Yet waited, to meld as I,
The bull demon
Desiring, desiring, desiring
My dark divine darling.

❂ LAKSHMI ❂

Between us
Let it be that space
Between the surf line and the shore
The Moon and the cool moonlight.
The Sun and harsh Sun rays
Stating Summer's here
The Hive and the honey
The Conch and the hushed
Whispers of the sea.

The forest and the dark floor
Showing up black under the tree canopy
The anklet and the dancer
Making rhythm out of silences
The mother and her child
Growing secretly under her heart.
Youth and the mad rush
Of a summer romance ushered in
By rampant hormones.
The smile of a child and butterflies
Sprinkling beauty in the air.
The elephant and his mahout
Who calls him, his eldest born.
The spade and the Earth,
Gracefully exposing its womb
Being fertilised, pushing out
Green shoots from the brown Earth
The wind and the myriad
Fragrances piggybacking on it
The lover and the breathy embrace
Where no one sees them.

Yes Kaali between you
And he who loved you
The way I do in this reincarnation
This Mahishaa turned human.

❁ MAHISHAA ❁

Yes I should have known better.

Turned away from you,
When I could have
Before my Soul caught up
With my heart, already ensnared
By your sweet song
Outside my fort, that I had built
To keep the likes of you away.

You are a threat to my wellbeing.

How could ALL of them be wrong?
My friends, well-wishers
My men in arms, who had battled
With me shoulder-to-shoulder
Letting me win on their valour
Asking for nothing in return
Except proximity to a warrior like me?
Many of them told me the truth
That I was definitely making a mistake
One which could cost me my life,
Let alone my kingdom.

No, the piddling Devas claimed.
That they were eager to maintain
Their positions of relevance
As my men; for only if I won
Would they get the respect
They seemed to be used to now.
They could not bear my risking myself
That too to a blithely singing woman
Riding a lion, controlling her mount
With just her thighs.

See, even my language is getting
Coloured by what is in me for you
Yes, I wanted this vast kingdom
And I got it, I fought for it.
Now I desire you with a fervour
I never really had to this extent
For my battles.
My love or lust or desire
Shows even in my silences
My exhalations are stronger, deeper
Than the air I inhale
When all I wanted was to inhale
The fragrance of a handful of your hair.
It's okay, once born death is inevitable.
No weapon could kill me I was certain
But your glance, glancing off my eyes
I see a fathomlessness in it
Reminding me of the black endlessness
Of death, now a welcome respite
To my love-battered heart slowly slowing
Stilling itself by your command!

❈ LOVE SONG ❈

Darling quaffer of blood
Eater of entrails
Why grab
When I am all too ready
To gift you my body
As a larder
For your appetite?

They shuddered at your blackness
Your terrifying laugh
Your bone jewellery
Clacking against each other
Your wild dance
They never looked
Deep into your eyes
Where the hunger for being
Loved

For yourself
Not despite it, lurked.

Dark love of mine
Come to me
Make me yours
Just the way you are.
I would not have you
Any other way
Not well-spoken, well-dressed
Your battle scars
On your tender body
Show you to be well lived
The blush on your cheeks
Well loved.
The World can snigger
Pass snide comments
You are perfect
For me.

❈ WHEN ❈

When you get tired of being worshipped
For many causes, you can easily fulfil
With scarce a lift of your eyebrows
When the flowers heaped at your feet
Dry out, exuding no more fragrance
When the Sanskrit shlokaas mispronounced
By priests who eye the Dakshina more than you
Hurt your ears, and when the gold
They put on you in ornament-shaped chains
Restrict you, constrict you
Then come to me, rest your head
On my pelt chest, my misshapen face above yours.

My breath the only prayer to you
My heart beat that rhythm you will dance to
On dark Amaavasya nights
My arms around you, your only jewellery.
Come beloved
I have not loved you for births
My births were only those times
You made me aware of my love for you.

❈ SUMMER NAVARATHRI 2020 ❈

It's the same old drama for nine days
That comes round twice a year.

I have asked you to be my queen
As you are already my love.
Your voice outside my fort seduced me
You taught me that love could occur
With people yet unseen.

You taught me many things
Yet I failed to teach you to love me
Failed further to stop loving you
Even though I knew too well
How it would conclude, each time.

But this Navarathri, no one will come
To see you all bedecked like a bride
Your Thrishul piercing my chest
When your refusal of my love
Had already annihilated me.

The priests are careless in the poojas
They will get no Dakshinas
No devotees to clutch their feet
And rest their head on them
So come, sit by me and chat awhile.

Yes, of course you can kill me
On the ordained ninth day
But till then, let me inhale your fragrance
Caress you with my eyes
Maybe catch a swift reflection
Of my bull visage in your shuttered eyes.

This crowd-less Navarathri, be mine
For a few moments let me LIVE
Before I happily die, sans you.

❈ **KAALI** ❈

So you made me, not because you loved me.

I was to do your bidding for you in exchange
Much like sons are bloodlines carrying your DNA.
What's preventing you from doing penance
With his intensity, or was that never for Gods?
Demons could worship, human beings entreat
But you Divinities can't deign to work for strength.
Take away my eyes Sun and Moon
Blind me that I may not see you cowering.
I fling my jewellery to the ground, let the Earth
Cover it up with dirt, my silken robes I discard.
My hair unbound that Yama gave, chop it off
Take away my myriad weapons, I'll take my chances
With him, if he kills me, it's okay, he says he cares
And I believe him, more than all of you Gods.

I shall retain only the lion I ride on to him
It's my father's gift to me and he just wants
Me to be happy, I know that he'll understand
He you call a demon – I have no fight with him.

You understand manipulations flattery, bribes
Love is alien to you, as alien as you are to me.
The world has lost a Goddess, let it be.
It's a fair barter, where I have gained a love.

❀ MAHISHAA SATHVIC ❀

Where's the doubt?

We were adversaries
Pitted against each other
In the battle of the Gods
Who hated losing
Especially to bull faced demons
Even as they extol cows,
Bathing themselves
With bovine urine
And hogging milk products.

But you, my love
With gentle eyes
And handheld weaponry
To make up an armoury
Why were you so different?
You ate flesh, drank blood
Left your thick hair loose
And laughed terrifyingly.
Blood and sweat smeared
Your skin shone like
The night sky with no moon
And stars dissolved into it.

You smelt of flowers
Wafting in summer breezes
Your voice was the sound
In the womb of the Ocean.
Seeing you, I forgot
The mewling Gods
With their petty worlds.
All I wanted was to sit by you
That very thought makes me
Absurdly happy
I sought that joy with you.
You, for reasons of your own
I do not need to know
Denied me that
And went about killing me.
Death at your hands
Was far better than a Life
Without you.

It's done and dusted
Then why remind me,
Revive me for these nine days
Two times a year
Just to torture me
With my love for you
That refused to die
With my demon body?

❖ PROXIMITY ❖

It is a bad idea to love Divinities
They are used to Worship.
A duality, a certain distance
That ensures that no one gets hurt
Beyond a point....
Something not just strange
But alien to lovers.

Where was the you
Where was the me, in 'Us'?
There are no safety nets
One-way valves, no limits
Which is bad, I guess.

But where was the ecstasy
A half smile will elicit
The fragrance of your exhalation
The sound of your breath
In the silence, the sweetness
Of your speech as you break it?
Your imagined touch
Is Paradise, something I can
Live on for weeks
Your executing me
Was a mere technicality.

While it may have been
A great thing for the Gods
I have never worshipped you
My dark love, only adored you
From that distance you demanded
Your joy was mine
Before I died I knew
What it was to love
Something you learned
Only after I was gone.

❀ FIGHT ❀

I cannot sleep these nights my love.

The thought of seeing you again
For tomorrow's battle keeps me up.

The sun glints off your jewellery
You wear no armour I notice
A very wrong dress code
For this conflict, unless you were sure
My weapons would not harm you.
Sometimes I feel you know everything
About me and my love for you
And sometimes I feel you have
Associated too much with the Gods
To allow any sense into your cognition.

My well-wishers warned me about you.
They have my best interests at heart
I know, for they vehemently disagree
With me, they try to dissuade me
From talking about you in private
They grimace when I drift off
To thoughts about you.

To be fair, they were less concerned
About themselves, when I lose to you,
If I lose to you, I mean
Than about what will happen to me.
They think I have been bewitched
By my greatest enemy, a woman to boot.

My darling I have lost my battle
For your love, the disdain on your face
Convinces me of that.
Does that mean my slumped shoulders
Tell you of my surrender?
I have crowned you Empress of my heart
My holdings are that of your vassal
You can refuse my love, but not
The sight of you facing me
Across the tumult of war.
My armies and yours fight
For supremacy of my hoards
Or the band of Gods, hiding behind you.

I fight to win you, your acquiescence
To me is good enough an answer
To the way you have possessed me
My deadly lover, my beautiful adversary.

Mahishaalakshmi

So much planning had gone into our scheme. Kaali had a vision that was all-encompassing. She had the advantage over Space and Time. She never forgot the tiniest detail too.

We wanted the whole action to be a single organic movement. There could be no slip ups, no replays. The whole world was going insane. Religion was taking leaps and bounds away from Spirituality. It had become Draconian. Most of the original religious texts were lost to antiquity or could be properly accessed only by a miniscule group of scholars. Many of them never cared to exit, or exist out of their world of Knowledge. The others had no compunction in using their scholarship for dubious ends. Sadly, the commonly available interpretations of these books read like Do-it-Yourself anarchy manual.

The secret cornerstone for religion became money, plain and simple. The growth of a group or sect was directly proportional to the wealth it could gather. There were huge, opulent places of worship which looked like a nine-tiered Hollywood wedding cake! There was room for everything there, with the probable exception of Divinity.

The very gates of the places of worship were heavily carved and imposing. There was evidently no easy passage in or out. They were obviously guarding something of great value, which was inside rather than outside. There were steel shelves to hold footwear. Little metal tokens hung on a bar. One boy who manned the kiosk was playing games on his mobile phone. The other was busy cleaning his teeth with one of the metal tokens. Both of them behaved to their customers as if they themselves were zombies.

There was an exquisitely woven silk carpet on the floor in black, white and red. There were unevenly shaped orange blossoms on it where people had spit the Paan from their mouths. Countless bare feet had ground it into the fabric very well.

Every shrine had a huge 'donation' box in front of it prominently placed so that while looking at the Deity inside, people were prone to stumble over it. The poorest of the poor of the country came and stood there, with folded hands and streaming eyes. They dug up a coin from somewhere within their voluminous clothes and dropped it reverentially into the hundi, as the donation box was called.

They were actually seeing their beloved Deities in front of them and it was an unbelievable joy! This was the way they had imagined them to be first, in their childhood stories, the dances and dramas in their village and finally on colour TVs. These simple villagers fell at the dirty feet of the priests there, believing them to have unique access to the Gods they tended. The priests had realised long ago that there was no money to be squeezed out of these people. They settled for ego massages, as the visitors fell reverentially at their feet. The villagers felt a kinship with the walking, talking tangible priests more than they did with the idol in the temples, which were just a step closer than their appearances on the television!

The priests knew how to milk the rich and the influential people who came to the temple. All of them, like most other people, had problems. It started with not having a son, or, secondarily a daughter. Then it was the children's health. The problem then became their education. The kids were not interested in their lessons and they were far too interested in activities the parents could not approve of, were they aware of it. Smoking, drugs, fast cars being driven recklessly etc in very bad company was quite common. Then came sexual entanglements. After navigating all these it was hard to find the child a job. Favours were called in. Influence and money was used. Having got a job, with such difficulties, the child seemed to have absolutely NO responsibility at all! Then came the big question of marriage. The family had to be right: a rough parity of wealth and social status was welcome. The would-be spouse would have to be educated, smart, home loving (which was a very interesting concept all in itself). Most of all, especially in the case of brides, docile. Having grown up seeing the rude way in which her mother was treated by her father, gave her a basic mistrust of men. She was defensive from the beginning. Her in-laws would be overbearing, adamant to set the tone from the very beginning! Had there been the slightest softening of attitudes on either side, it could always have been a different story.

The apt solution for all these problems were the priests and the venue for it was the temple. The priests solemnly nodded their heads and recommended pooja after expensive pooja. These priests served the job of a psychiatrist or psychologist. They were people one could vent on to every day! Like the most expensive 'mind doctors', these priests did not also come cheaply. The temple and its Deities became mere props in the drama of both the rich visitor's lives and less forgivably the priests' life.

There was an even bigger but silent scam. Scamsters caught on to the fact that religion was a huge money spinner. After conferring with each other the charlatans made themselves heads of sects. They took the concept of Divinity and chopped it up into juliennes of lies. They wrested Truth from God. All the Gods were muzzled by the ambition of these 'spiritual heads'.

They guaranteed that love, cleanliness, service, charity, joy, acceptance and inclusivity were far, far away from the human beings who trusted them. The devotees and the priests were equally alien to love, which was supposed to be the primary concept in the places of worship they were in. Any place of worship was to give food for the needy. Shelter from the elements, a place to clean themselves, to study basic language, mathematics etc was the original idea of these structures that housed Divinity.

EVERY religion averred that God was omnipresent. There was actually no need for demarcated residences for God or Gods. What was sad was the most valuable of residences of all Divinities – the human hearts and minds – were fast being closed down. It was becoming okay, even preferable, to relegate these Gods into structures made of cement, stone and wood. Huge amounts were paid in the construction of these abodes of the Supreme Energies.

This made it possible for Gods to be substituted by Godmen, with definite agendas of their own.

It was childishly easy to create a fight and stoke the hatred, till it grew under its own weight to smother everything that was decent! A dead cow in the well of the Hindu quarter, a dead pig on the mosque steps, a love affair of a lonely Mother Superior, all these were used as weapons against believers of the other faith. Some hired thugs (common to all sections) were paid to start a skirmish. Fez caps, ochre cloths etc were used judiciously as the case may have been. Holy ash, wooden crosses, books like the Bible, Bhagavatham and Quran were distributed generously. Sadly, no one read these books. Their use was almost exclusively as props to religious fights.

There was a property that human blood had that was beyond Biology. If it had been spilt in a conflict, it had a tendency to inundate the minds of MANY people. The sticky, metallic red blood became raging fires of the minds. There was no logical reason for this anger. But there was no way to douse these furious flames, except by oblations of more quantities of the very same blood.

The easiest way to make money and accumulate power was to get human beings to maim if not kill each other. There was no thought, let alone guilt, for these man-made horrors. The greater the atrocities, bigger the fear. More and more people banded together not out of common interests but out of despair. They thought that their safety lay in large groups. Unfortunately, these groups were led by people who did not have the least compunction to kill a few of their own group and blame the others for it. Nobody had the courage or compassion to suo moto halt this! Each sect waited in vain for the 'Others' to make the first move towards reconciliation.

The politicians understood the simplicity of such manipulations. There were huge but secret conclaves of the so-called spiritual leaders and political leaders. They understood and admired each other. They also protected each other. The differences among them were purely technical. They needed each other. A major fight once a year, with two, three minor ones kept them in business. Their followers were bound together in suspicion, fear and hatred. Such groups could be moulded with the greatest of ease.

Instead of following true Divinities, human beings were actively encouraged to follow these devils in human form, oozing fake piety! Exclusion, punishment, alienation, hate, trickery, greed and power games were all part of it. Many innocent human beings were led astray. Some of the cleverer ones ran away from the whole system. The scoundrels who were the so-called political and spiritual leaders saw to it that they were ostracised and driven far away from the majority of ordinary society. The ONLY thing in their favour was that the lies and hate they spread were far too weak to survive against the slightest of positivity! Even when riding on top of their power-mad tsunamis, these people were worried that the Ocean would suddenly dry up.

THIS was the one set of people who Kaali was deadly against! She could see in them real evil, the kind of which She was not familiar with despite Her numerous battles with demons. Kaali first wanted to expose this horridness for what it actually was. Then She was confident that the vast majority of people would shun it. But for that, She had to show up the Truth for what it really was!

Our idea was to establish what was real and good first. Other things could be worked out later on.

Kaali had discussed the whole issue threadbare with me.

Each time I saw Her, I found myself distracted by Her beauty. Her fragrance was so sweet and subtle that it was only when She left that I realised just what I had been inhaling. From the glazed look on my face, Kaali could comprehend what my state was! Sometimes, She repeated things intently, checking all the time whether I was listening properly. During other times, She would gently stroke my head and I found vistas of knowledge opening out in me. What was wonderful was that I was able to recollect every bit of it at will!

Kaali's epic fight with Mahishaa was well known. The dramatis personae were well established. There was Kaali the Supreme. She was the combined Energy of EVERYTHING. Mahishaa was pitted against Her. Mahishaa's fault lay in that he was a nonconformist.

He was not ready to 'box' people, stick a label on them and then proceed to treat them according to what was written on the label. As he was not part of any group, they all found it easy to gang up against him, certain that there would be no one to defend him.

Mahishaa's greatest sin was to choose Love over everything else! It had taken the mob a long time and a lot of effort to obliterate love from the consciousness of a lot of people. Love was so potent that this single action of Mahishaa's would topple their efforts in an instance! They could not – would not – let Mahishaa survive.

Mahishaasura

As stated before, things were extremely well discussed and settled between Kaali and me. There were no areas of doubt.

I was to don on the role of Mahishaa and She would be my Mahishaasuramardini. It would be a one-to-one battle. There were no people of the calibre of the old Mahishaa's troops in valour OR heinousness. It was as if committing the sins too had become timorous! But then, Kaali set forth a counter-condition. She was with me. She would always be with me.

I was to carry out our mutually-decided plan. But She, Kaali, would vanish from the bandwidth of my vision, hearing, smell, taste and touch till She came to claim me as Her's and carry me away! This was the price I had to pay to get Her. I had to move forward on Faith alone.

She used to share small red sour sweet fruits with me. They were smaller than raisins. I had gotten used to Her soft fingers in my hair, Her fragrant breath on me. Her laugh and the sound of Her golden anklets were the same. I loved the way they hung low on Her feet. Sometimes She let me stick my fingers under them. They had beautiful golden bells on them and each bell rang true. She said that there were a Thousand bells on each anklet! I loved the deep colours She wore, always with a tasteful gold border. Her jewellery, like Her weapons, were exquisitely crafted. As a treat She let me wind myself wholly in Her hair. 'Shirt of Hair!', I would chuckle with Her.

Sometimes She would let me bathe Her. Her oil had to be heated just so. Sometimes She would show me the Yoga aasanas She had learnt from Shiva. Her body was dark and so wonderfully toned. Her skin, flesh, muscles and bones used to move in perfect tandem. She was easily one of the best dancers I had seen. There was a story that Shiva and She entered into a dance competition. Soon it was just the two of Them dancing to see Who would win. Whatever Shiva did, She would better it and dance. With a tiny smile She would egg on Shiva. In despair Shiva did a straight upward split. Kaali paused. It was not that Her body could not copy this. She was hesitant to do this in front of all the Gods. Yelling triumphantly, Shiva was declared to be the Nataraja or the Lord of Dance. It was rumoured that Shiva came to Kaali in person and surrendered to Her superior craft. When I questioned Her on this, She just smiled Her maddeningly secretive smile, as She had been reputed to do, all those aeons ago!

I had steadfastly loved Kaali, from what I suspected was births ago. Oh yes, there was a time when I believed in NO Divine Powers. There was no trace of resentment in Her, when I told Her about all that.

'It was not yet time!', She averred. Coming from the very controller of Time, it was rich! But that was what was special about Her. She cared tremendously. But Her love was vast and it let me totally free. Despite the laughable power proportions between Her and me, She let me set the rules. Sometimes when She slept, or was engrossed in the affairs of the Universe, I used to sneak a glance at Her and marvel at Her simplicity. God WAS love. And the most perfect of loves was Her's!

So even though She had told me that She would be an undeniable presence in my life, this was the very first time that She left me, without the dubious endorsement of my Five senses after our talk on the steps. This was hell for me.

I WAS starting to miss Her. What my brain clinically acknowledged to me, my heart was definitely not going to agree with it! I roundly cursed those who devalued the worth of the Five senses. What did THEY know about Her beauty, Her subtle fragrance, Her sweet voice, Her tender skin and the divine taste of the things She brought for me from Her realm. Sometimes, Her fingers brushed my lips and I involuntarily pursed them to kiss Her.

I found myself muttering away to Kaali with the complete hope that She was always listening in. But hoping was very different indeed from believing! I was straining to have some kind of physical proof that She was adhering to Her promise. It was preposterous not to trust Kaali's word, given directly to me. But such was my human frailty. If a human-Divine bond was not easy, what then about a demon-Divine bond?

Kaali Herself had confirmed that it was indeed Mahishaa who had loved Her the most. With the non-appearance of Kaali in my daily life, I was dwelling a lot more on Mahishaa, beyond what was commonly known.

I found myself getting restless and irritated at the slightest thing. I went to temple after temple. Most of them were gorgeous. Some of them were powerful centres of spiritual strengths. Yet, I was missing the frequent and physical presence of Kaali in my life, however much She kept on assuring me of Her interest in me, in my mind. Trapped in my body, it was not easy for me to make the transition into the metaphysical realm.

Seemingly randomly, I decided to go to those very temple steps where Kaali and I had sat and chatted a good while ago.

I used to look keenly at the steps each time I passed them. There was absolutely no trace of anything out of the ordinary having happened there. Yet, for me those steps were as sacred as the sanctum sanctorum of the temple. I wished that I didn't have to tread on them to reach Her abode. Each time I protested, amused She used to ask me whether there was ANYTHING and ANYWHERE which was barred to Her! It was impossible to argue with Her and win.

This was the night of Amavasi or the New Moon. The Earth could not see even a sliver of the Moon on this night. Consequently, the stars appeared to be brighter and bigger as well as much closer to the Earth. Even a thin crescent of the Id ka Chaand or the Moon that sanctioned the breaking of the Ramzaan fast, made the stars look duller. Whether the Moon's light was borrowed from the Sun or not, there was something magical about it. Everyone forgave the moods of the Moon. Its unearthly beauty made up for a lot of its unsteadiness!

Quietly I made my way up the steps and plonked myself down. The stone still retained the warmth of the Sun. It was really very late at night. The wind seemed to have turned in for the night.

The only sound was that of Kalidasan steadily chomping on his greenery. There was a distant rustling of grass. It could have been snakes or tiny creatures of the night going about their business. The whippet-thin pack of stray dogs which loitered around the temple premises did not seem to be there.

Looking North-Eastwards, I could feel tears pouring down my cheeks. My face was inscrutable. But I did nothing to check my tears.

'Take it, take it as an Abhishekam to you!', I thought viciously. 'You accept EVERYTHING. Take this. The salt in my tears will be a good exfoliant for you.' There was no love, no devotion in me then. I was desperately missing Her. THAT was my mood.

Gently, I could sense the darkness around me becoming denser. The stars overhead were getting blotted out. Yet, I could see no clouds. For a second, utter joy filled me. Not daring to make any sudden move which would have upset Her, I softly called out 'Kaali?'

There was so much wealth of longing in my voice. Bhakthavalsala or She who would take care of Her devotees was yet another of Her many, many names.

THE darkness near me stopped moving. I could feel a great warmth coming from it.

'Who are you? Show yourself! Don't play with little light there is!', I said sharply. Somehow, I was sure nothing would – and could – hurt me on Her temple steps.

There was a sigh like the snoring of a resting storm wind.
'I am Mahishaa.'

Mahishaa! On these very steps Kaali had sat with me and convinced me that it WAS indeed Mahishaa who had loved Her the most. I remembered Her eyes, the urgency of Her tone, Her grip on my hand. Did that happen yesterday or aeons ago? Both, I felt sometimes.

'Mahishaa!', my voice came out thick with tears.

'May I sit?', asked Mahishaa.

I nodded. Instinctively Mahishaa climbed three steps below me, not sitting where Kaali had sat. All I could see was a large area of absolute blackness.

So much like HER skin, I thought.

'Where is Kaali?', I asked shortly. I wanted to know. Yet I would have been dismayed if Mahishaa had been with Her when I was not.

'Waiting for you', said Mahishaa.

A great load of sadness lifted from me. Was She too waiting... waiting the way I was? Wanting to meet me? Eager to meet me, even? For the first time in days I smiled into the night. My heart was full of affection for this dark creature whose answer had soothed me. Besides, I was prejudiced in Mahishaa's favour after what Kaali had declared about his love for Her.

Waves of warmth rose from Mahishaa. I could also smell the earthy fragrance off him. It was powerful, but totally natural. It was a smell I could trust. Many people had accused me of having animalistic reactions. I found that I was better off trusting those, rather than any studied responses.

'You have agreed to reenact our story, have you not?', Mahishaa asked with great kindness.

'You are sure, are you not, that you still want to go through it? You can still opt out of it. There is time yet!', continued Mahishaa softly.

'Why did YOU not opt out?. She gave you many chances. She never lied to you. She said She would HAVE to kill you. Complete disclosure! Still you chose death. Why?', I asked him. This was something which I had wanted to clarify from someone for a long time. Who better than Mahishaa himself to tell me the truth!

'Because I love Her so much! Beyond life. Without Her by me there is NOTHING that I want, nothing I need.'

There was no drama in Mahishaa's declaration. The words he used were the wondrous ones; his tone was even.

'Do you have the time or the interest to hear my story?' he asked.

I nodded. I remembered how I had told Kaali that I love stories on these very steps. I wanted to shake the old stone steps to set them remembering that. Kaali had sat here. Did not the steps consider themselves to be special? Kaali was said to be there in everything, living and inanimate.

'MY father was a great warrior and a demon. Along with his brother he did incredible penances and got great power. When he had obtained his boons, he saw my mother. She was beautiful and one of the first females he saw. He made love to her and I was born. It did not matter to my mother that my father was a demon. Nor did it matter to my father that she was a cow. She was beautiful. Her name was Shyamala. They loved each other. I looked like my mother; but had my father's physique. They adored me. The Devas HATED anyone with power. They constantly squabbled among each other. But they presented a united front to their enemies. All of them united to kill my father and his brother. Distraught, my mother chose not to live without him and jumped into his funeral pyre. They left me alone on this Earth.

'It was the kind hearted tree Spirits who brought me up. They needn't have done it. But they were like my mother and father rolled into one. They told me stories about my father's valour – of that of my uncle too. They spoke glowingly of the love my parents shared. They spoke of my mother's gentleness. They kept the memory of my blood parents in me. They were careful not to fan hatred for the Devas in me. They had seen too much blood being shed. They did not want me to be involved with yet another fight with the Devas.'

There was a pause.

'However, I felt I was letting them down if I did not question the Devas at least. I sought them out. Yet, they would never answer me. It was either I was too small, too weak and they were too great and capable to take me seriously. Some of them I came across when they were alone were not so obnoxious. But in a group, they were insufferable. My curiosity turned into anger and then naturally hatred! They were the assassins of my parents and they treated me as if I were of no consequence.'

Mahishaa was lost in his past.

'One day, I just left. The kind tree Spirits would have tried to dissuade me. They had made sure that I was taught proper fighting and I knew myself to be quite good at it. It was not that they had thought being namby-pamby was acceptable. They did not want one more generation fighting the Devas. They, and the Earth they were standing on, had smelt the rankness of spilt blood once too often.'

'I went deep into the forest where sunlight came from eleven to two in the daytime. My sky was the thick green treetops. For a month I foraged on vegetation. Then on water. Finally, air. All I wanted was power! Power to do what I wanted to do. Do you remember your school physics lessons? Power is the ability to do work. No one was with me. Only my deep desire to get what I wanted kept me going. Time stopped for me. I was just one moment and I was filled with determination to be the best, forever!'

I nodded again. Mahishaa sometimes spoke like Kaali, I thought. Her words, his style of delivery.

'Bit by bit I got access to the different weapons and their arcane Manthras. Warfare was not just a physical thing. It was body, heart, mind, soul all looking intently at victory. That was the only way to win a war. When I had mastered these, I knew that I had to get the blessings of the Almighty.

'For the time being, I forgot all that I had gained in weaponry. I went back to being a novice at meditation. I was meditating on the Ultimate Energy, nameless, formless yet the greatest there was. By then I had become used to honing my entire self to a goal. It seemed that I had closed my eyes. When I opened it one of the most effulgent of Beings was smiling before me. Naturally I asked for Power. I asked to be Immortal and to be undefeated by anyone. I was careful to cover all possible assailants in that list.

'Immortality was not available to any living thing. A birth meant a certain death. However, rather craftily I asked for – and got – protection from almost all entities. However, 'woman' was not on my list! Smilingly (possibly relieved) I was given the rest of the things I had requested.

'I had never been with a woman. I had seen the special bond between my parents. Women, as a species, did not exist for me. Their shapes were mostly hidden from me. Their touch was totally alien to me.

'My first act as I got out of the forest which had been my Guru was to assemble an army. Nobody knew of me and only great-takers and mercenaries were with me. However, armed with the knowledge of my boons, I avoided the mercenaries and concentrated on those who seemed to have faith in me. Slowly, we won battle after battle. Larger, better-trained armies were falling to us. No one could face me in a one-to-one fight and win. Our reputation, size of the army and territories under us grew exponentially.

'The whole of this Earth was mine. The next world we took over was that of the Devas. The proud Devas found themselves being menials in the very places they had ruled. It amused me to make their erstwhile slaves their bosses. I would deliberately order the Devas to serve the demi-Gods, far below them in hierarchy. It would make both parties uncomfortable and that was very enjoyable. Whenever I saw them cringe, it assuaged a little bit of my pain of losing my parents so senselessly.

'I started my womanising days with the frail wives of the Devas. I waited till their delicate daughters would wed one of the Devas. Very often before the husband had touched her, I would ravish her! The male Devas lost their honour and the ladies were scarred for life! They could never settle down to a normal life ever again. Soon enough, I became an adept lover.

'It was the bold apsaras who were not afraid of me who started to dominate me in bed and teach me first how to pleasure myself and then, them! I lost my wish to take women by force. I learned about the subtler battles of the psyche and wanted to win in THAT arena.

'Still, throughout every activity of mine, I continued my Saadhana or practice diligently. Armed by my boon, I did not have to behave decently. I could get away with uncouthness. But there was no one for me, with me. I worked hard and got ample fruits of that labour. Of course, there were people who admired me, respected me. There were people who were on my side as they felt I was always a winner. But love? My parents and those Tree Spirits had truly loved me. I carried them within me like a beautiful and secure cave I could retreat into, safely.'

Mahishaa paused. Like the almost- automatic change in Kaali's tone and demeanour, Mahishaa too changed before my very eyes.

Mahishaa's words had touched me. His battles had been fairly fought and hard won.

LOOKING at Mahishaa, I felt myself melting into a bottomless pond of love and desire much like him! THIS was the one who had loved Kaali unreservedly. He had heard Her sing, sent envoys to Her. His people had been massacred by Her. He had fought Her too. She had repeatedly asked him to leave and be the king of the nether world. He had agreed to give up the kingdom of the Devas, just because She had wanted him to do so.

It was not a wily quid pro quo deal for him. He loved Kaali. Wanted proximity to Her. Without that he opted to die. She was what was vital for him. Staying alive was not the important thing. Living on certain chosen terms was what was crucial to him and he had chosen to either be close to Her or not be! Mahishaa had not made wild declarations of love and then petered things down so that no one would insist that he actually carry out what he had threatened to do.

There was no anger in him for Kaali. She, in fact, was the one who had blanched when Mahishaa had asked Her one question. Was there any need for Her to have instilled SUCH love in him, if She was anyway going to kill him?

Mahishaa was fully aware of the extent of power he had gathered into himself. Obviously Kaali was much more powerful than that, which made Her into one of the omnipotents of Creation. In the various lectures and discussions Mahishaa had taken part in, everyone had come to the conclusion that there was a hidden Energy in everything and this Energy occasionally appeared in different forms. Confident persons were able to revere their own Divinity and at the same time respect those of the others, irrespective of whether they believed in them or not.

Conflict between worthy warriors raised the level of the battle to heroic levels. There was an intrinsic difference of quality between a suicide bomber and someone who lit the fuse of a bomb from far away. The result of the detonation was hateful and unwelcome in both cases, no doubt. Still the bravery of the two attackers were at two levels naturally.

Mahishaa had known the day Kaali had hummed a primal 'Hum' which decimated his commander Dhoomravilochanan and his army that the lady who rode a lion and sang so sweetly outside his fort, was indeed his Nemesis.

Old memories of not being protected from death in the hands of a woman rose in him. He was prepared to die, if his time was up. He knew that those who lived by the sword would, one day, die by it! The only thing he had not factored in was his falling totally in love with Her, who almost certainly was the one going to kill him. The warrior in Mahishaa was prepared to die in a battle. The male in Mahishaa had not been prepared to fall in love with anyone, let alone his adversary.

I asked Mahishaa the one question which was uppermost in my mind.

'Was it hard to die for love, harder than just normal dying?'

Mahishaa held his breath for a long time.

'Dying was easy. Not getting to spend time with your beloved was the hard thing!'

'See …we know that we are born, that we will die; one day. Nothing here is permanent. But within this golden impermanence, we seek things which make us happy. I know, sages say that one should be indifferent to both unhappiness and happiness. But we seem to gravitate to the latter. Knowing everything. My father – and mother – whose deaths I was avenging by

attacking the Devas were not there to see my victory. It did not matter to them in the least. It did not bring them back to me. Yet, I did it!'
I nodded. I understood exactly what he had meant by that.

'Sure, I enjoyed my conquests. All of them! But once I was made aware of Her; that was it. Her presence made all the difference between joy and mere victory.' Mahishaa looked at me deeply for a moment.

'Are you certain that you want to reenact our story? That too, as me', he asked me quietly.

'May I ask you a question?', I asked Mahishaa in return.

'Did you ever regret meeting Her, even for a moment?'

Mahishaa laughed a deep laugh that had a component which was a sob in it.

'Never! Even if I had the choice of living my Life all over again, I would do the same! Maybe I would have been gentler to those weaker than me. But no, with Her my choice would have been the same. It will be the same too, birth after birth', he said.

He had just confirmed what I had instinctively known.

'Mahishaa, I am ready to die for Her. She can use me, abuse me, misuse me, She can do anything with me to teach Her Creation all about love. So long as I mingle with Her. So long as I am able to Love, so long as there IS love in my life, so long as She loves me, it is okay. She loved you, did She not? She took your Pranaa into Her!'

'Lakshmi!', said Mahishaa, 'I believe you. I believe that you are the one to be Her own Mahishaa this birth. Come, let me teach you how to die!'

Mahishaa ran his eyes over me and hugged me. He ran his cloven foot all over me. I felt that I was being caressed by my grandmother. I felt such a sense of security by his side.

'You know that She and I battled it out. How do you propose to die?', he asked me. 'There are no more pitched battles of the kind we had. If you want your viewers to know all about love, conflict and death, the fact that you are fighting has to be made clear.'

WE discussed many methods. The one I favoured was the actual Rakthapushpanjali, mentioned in the Granthams. I would slice my veins, dip a jasmine flower into my blood for each of Her names and do pooja to Her. Mahishaa rightly vetoed it. Most people would think that I had gone mad and then committed suicide and then they would go on to blame Kaali for not protecting me from such thoughts, for my love for Kaali was well known and people would think that She had let me down.

My body had to be destroyed and what was left had to merge with Her. What about an illness which insidiously took over my body? I was game for that. Like the wounds which had bloomed on Mahishaa's body, the illness would hurt me. Cancer was the most obvious one. It suited my psycho-profile too. My father's mother had given me her love for poetry. Long ago, she passed away from cancer. My father had made the extremely brave and considerate decision not to have her treated when it was clear that with treatment and a lot of pain, she may have survived for eight months or so and without it she would have succumbed in half a year. She had died within four months. There was a sense of aptness about the whole thing.

Mahishaa told me in a soft voice. 'If you are ready, I can fill you with my essence.'

I nodded.

'When will I see Her again? Now? After you finish?', I asked him eagerly.

'Soon. Very soon', he said.

He ran his hands over me. I could feel tiny icy particles enter me. They settled in me, nesting in places which stung me a little.

'I am you', said Mahishaa.

'And She is us!', I whispered. The delight in both of us would have washed Her feet.

She would have to move those very feet step by step towards me and claim me publicly. Mahishaa's forbidden passion was coming into play again. However many times She killed him for each Navarathri, She could never really annihilate his love for Her. I was yet one more proof of this Eternal Truth!

'You will not see me anymore, except when you look into your own eyes in a mirror. Stay in Her!'

Mahishaa hugged me once more and I fancied that I had inhaled Her fragrance after a long time. I do not remember how I reached home. I felt full – as if I had swallowed a full Moon, still glowing gently in me.

Was there something strange in me when I woke up the next morning? There was always something strange about me! So nothing could differentiate what I was that day. The extra factor in me remained in me. But I had to start making people aware of Kaali and the love Mahishaa had for her! Their story was always talked about as a fierce battle to the finish!

OF course, everyone knew about the old Kaali temple which was now abandoned and all the lore attached to it.

Traditional Brahmins whispered among themselves of the stories they had heard from their ancestors. They spoke of goats being sacrificed in the temple Five times a year; for the Summer and Winter Navarathris as well as Her birthday and on the last day of the year and the first of the New year.

There were many legends about the Kaali there. She was in Her temple without ANY other Deities.

She was supposed to have slammed the temple door shut after someone had removed Mahishaa's statue from its position near Her feet. In fact, Mahishaa was the one who did pooja to Her behind closed doors. She would not deign to show Her face until Mahishaa returned or was returned to Her. She would kill the person whosoever opened Her sanctum-sanctorum doors. Her anger was so much! These were all diverse and well-known stories and I would have to skillfully weave my narrative into this.

Apropos nothing, I told those who I loved the most and who trusted me the most, that it was time to open the Kaali temple. She had waited long enough and was getting impatient. And yes, if She needed a human sacrifice, I was there, more than willing to feed Her, who had looked after me and all I loved so well. As the Cartoon channel would declare – it was payback Time.

The priests knew that it was far easier to manage worship at the Mahalakshmi shrine, so long as they limited the poojas and the Manthras of that particular shrine to be that of Shri Mahalakshmi who was interested only in wealth. They conveniently forgot that aspect of Her which dealt with the wealth of wisdom etc. They also were made to forget the whimsicality of Shri Mahalakshmi, by that very Deity Herself. She would give and withdraw good fortune in a moment!

The people who came there had one great desire that was common to all of them and that was money, money, money. This desire seemed to be contagious too. Each priest wore heavy gold jewellery on themselves. An average bride would be decked out similarly! The petitioners would bring the most expensive thing they could afford to lay their hands on and hand it over to the priests. Most of them had the mobile number of their favourite priests with them. They would call ahead and announce their arrival with all the number of people who could make it for the pooja as possible. The more the number of people, the greater the income as Dakshina.

There was a marked rivalry between the priests. Each of them wished to 'corner' a wealthy devotee. Poaching among the devotees was very common. But once the deal was done, there was great cooperation among the priests. A small cut of the Dakshina would be shared among all of them. The young acolytes with just down, rather than hair, on their faces would see the greed in the eyes of the older ones. They had to be content with wearing a thin gold chain for the time being. The glint of gold on the priests and the beautiful Deity of Shri Mahalakshmi shone brilliantly in the glare of electric lights recessed into the ceiling of the Sanctum Sanctorum.

Poojas were done according to the time available for the devotees. Abhishekam or the ritual bath was either done elaborately with each material, if the devotees had time. If not, all the unguents were poured into a vessel, mixed well and poured on the Deity's head. The colour of this was a pinkish yellow. The sari usually given by those who had booked an Abhishekam would be draped elegantly on the Mahalakshmi idol. The priests were better at pleating the heavy silk than many women who wore them! The Goddess' heavy jewellery would be put on her. Sometimes the rim of her gem encrusted crown would sit oddly on her forehead. No one bothered.

They would bring in buckets and buckets of varieties of rice, milk products, fruits, payasam etc. The vessels would be thrown in front of her. The main priest who took out a portion of the consecrated food to put it in her mouth would have black filth under his nails. Dried blood would be on his cuticles that he had nibbled on. Without washing his hands, he would rub them on his mundu and with sticky fingers do the Aarathi. All the priests had perfected the art of bellowing out the incantations. In that general cacophony, even those who were not sure of the words could adlibb quite convincingly!

The devotee would give a vacant smile at the Goddess and fall fervently at the priest's feet. In a ponderous voice the priest would say that things would be alright three or four months hence and that the devotee was to come back and repeat the pooja, once things worked out. The more enterprising of them offered to do 'mini poojas' for them once a month till good fortune smiled at them again. Everyone was happy. None of them cared to remember the Kaali shrine which was the oldest part of the temple. People under the age of twenty were not even aware of its existence.

People hesitated to go past that area even during the day, as the priests discouraged everyone from even remembering or thinking about the ancient Kaali there.

They had found a way of letting devotees off doing a complete circumambulation of the shrine, which would have automatically included the closed Kaali shrine too. They said it was quite sufficient to go around the golden flagstaff three times and put your head on the polished granite flower there. Nobody spoke about it. But gradually, the older part of the Kaali temple was treated as an area to be avoided by human beings.

The fat sweaty priests in the Mahalakshmi shrine said in phlegmy whispers that not even ants went into the locked shrine, no, not even when the priests left molasses and sugar and coconut and beaten rice in front of the old shrine. Opening it up for Navarathri once a year was a custom which had now been stopped.

The priests had all heard and spread various rumours about the Kaali who was enshrined and later on, enclosed, in the old part of the temple. Oral and written Sanskrit scrolls proved that this was the oldest part of the temple. There were nine huge bells just outside the shrine made of some metal, no one was able to identify. They shone like gold covered by clouds and their tone rang out clear and high when rung.

There were artefacts there which were too heavy and huge to be removed even by the sly antiquarians who scavenged dilapidated shrines throughout the land.

The more circumspect of them gave money as offerings in exchange to the Kaali there. To their chagrin they found that their monetary offerings seemed to have 'fallen through' the iron box called Hundi, placed before the Deity. There seemed to be an underground slit which endlessly swallowed all that was put in.

When the priests and the authorities, who thought that they were the ones taking care of the Kaali, rather than the other way around, scrabbled round through the little door flap at the side of the hundi, they found a thick layer of dust and nothing else! It seemed that Kaali was none too pleased about that exchange offer! When they tried to prise off the hundi from the floor, all nine bells had clanged out though there was nobody ringing them. The men had stopped their efforts instantly and left, locking the shrine carefully behind them.

The story went on that when the shrine was reopened, one of the metal wrenches they had accidentally left behind in their hurry to get out had turned into solid gold where it had been left on the floor. Some of the priests had reverentially placed it in one of Kaali's hands. There was a glow in the temple and all those who were there found a sudden upturn in their fortunes.

From starting to adore Kaali, the priests had started getting scared of Her! The older priests and the very young ones loved Her. 'Mai Ma', they used to affectionately call Her. Yet they were no match for the other kind of priests who had made Commerce their real God, albeit cleverly couched in other words.

The newer brand of priests first found out that they could not complete the pooja at the Kaali shrine, without the help of either the older priests or the very young ones. It embarrassed them no end when the three-year-old boy lisped out the complicated Sanskrit prayers without fault. The middle-aged priests could not complete the Sanskrit verses which were to accompany the pooja. The occasional devotees who still came to the Kaali temple then started abandoning the middle-aged priests for the very young or the very old ones, who were not obsessed about the Dakshina offered. This left the middle-aged priests red faced with embarrassment.

THE Kaali temple started to get a power all of its own, even when the sanctum sanctorum doors were shut. This was despite the best efforts of the priests and those who managed the Shri Mahalakshi shrine. All kinds of people still went there. The offerings varied from Tulsi and Thechchi garlands, to lotuses and jasmine. A sprig of flowers was enough. A ball of jaggery, a handful of rice, a vessel full of cow's milk etc was given joyfully, respectfully and the results were doubly so! There were people who swore that they had heard the heavy chime of a disembodied Deity's anklets, accompanied by deep, low growls of a lion. It had come from within the abandoned Kaali temple, they insisted.

It was at that time that the local politician along with the greedy priests devised a plan. The politicians were interested in money. People often gave generously in the name of God.

The priests were largely ignorant about the rituals in the temples they were serving in. As they were unsure of themselves, it was very easy for a 'group' to run the show. In the name of Democracy and equal importance for everybody, these sacred places were gradually becoming management – rather than Divinity-oriented!

They were to have a huge pooja there. The scrolls had said that the Goddess there was Mahishaasuramardini, fully armed with one leg on the Bull Demon looking up adoringly at Her, as he lay dying by Her weapons. There was no image of Mahishaasura there, though the priests used to worship the space by Her foot which was of a different colour.

These priests and the politician proclaimed that they were going to consecrate a golden idol of Mahishaasura, encrusted with diamonds and have it installed by Her feet. The traditional priests were aghast; Mahishaasura's presence was one that was taken for granted. His presence was all the more potent in his physical absence, they believed. One day the idol of Mahishaa would come back into the temple, which would re-energise the whole place again. But this loud and flashy way of doing it was not correct. It was faith not wealth and pomp which was lacking there.

Mahishaasura's total love was what made this Goddess incandescent with Energy. The traditional priests first begged their colleagues to stop this crazy idea. When they found them to be adamant, they went as a group to the politician's house. The man was dismissive of them. Weeping, his wife fell at their feet, begging them to stave off the catastrophe which was sure to follow. Playing with Divinity was a very dangerous pastime, one with fatal consequences. But the politician and the middle-aged priests were adamant about this.

TWO separate sets of activities happened in the Kaali temple. A simple lamp was lit in front of the Goddess and the very old priests and the very young ones started hymning Her. They were petitioning Her to forgive the others for their greed, to protect everyone with Her infinite Grace. They all knew that the diamond-studded Mahishaa's golden head was a ploy to collect illicit money! They intoned Her One Thousand Names, One Thousand Times.

An old Oracle was called in. He prostrated before Kaali and lay with his head on the cool floor for a long time. When he got up, his eyes were glazed over.

'Kaali is in one of Her violently playful moods! She is arranging for an actual proof... in these times... where there is no faith, only crowds shouting about Divinity... their hearts and minds closed. She will prove that Mahishaa, long considered a demon, Her enemy who fought Her... became one with Her. She will stop seeing people... She will stay inside Her closed doors... till someone comes who loves Her enough to give up her/his life for Her. Someone who WILL come. Someone whose intensity will shatter the stones and show Mahishaasuramardini to the world. There is NO Mahishaasuramardini without Mahishaa. Mahishaa is Her Leela, Her amusement. Did She really need Nine days to kill that demon She herself made?'

The Oracle was sweating and shivering as he said this. Once again he fell at Her feet. 'You have blessed me O Mother', he wept. 'I am in ecstasy. Let these words I have uttered before you come true. Kaalika! O Mother! Kindness personified! I surrender to Thee!' With many a backward glance the Oracle went out. The politician and his gang were waiting outside. The Oracle folded his hands to them.

'Please please leave Ammavari alone. She is very kind. So, we are all surviving. Do not test Her patience. Do not test Her love. Please, learned

Sirs. You do not know Her.' With tears streaming down his face, he left.

The day of the consecration of Mahishaa dawned with a clear sky. Throughout the night there was thunder and lightning through the rough papery air. The cloth covered statue of Mahisha was being rolled into the temple premises in elephant carts. The shrine of Kaali glowed with unearthly red light. There were growls of a lion emanating from within, which was heard by everybody assembled there and not just by those who believed in the Kaali there. Suddenly from the clear sky a bolt of lightning, immediately followed by thunder, hit the covered statue. It crumbled to bits. All those who were involved in this fell to the floor. They were writhing on the floor... chaos reigned.

Many were hurt, paralysed, maimed. En masse they fled. The older priests cleaned up as well as they could. The middle-aged ones were nowhere to be seen. Soon, about Thirty of them got together and closed the Kaali shrine. They vowed to cleanse themselves and reopen the shrine for Navarathri, a practice that had lasted for a few years till it tapered away. The Kaali temple stood majestically shut by the bustling temple of Shri Mahalakshmi.

There were many people gathering daily in the Shri Mahalakshmi temple. The predictions of the oracle was discussed over and over again. There was fear and confusion, two of the things which should never be associated with Divinity of any kind. People were scared of destruction, evil befalling them, death. Some were hopeful that Kaali would re-manifest Herself.

Many did not know what was to be done. Ignorance was a definite ingredient for fear. There was a lot of talk, a few constructive suggestions and a lot of rehashed gossip. Everyone agreed that SOMETHING had to be done to propitiate that Kaali. No one seemed to agree on what was to be done though!

After listening to days of chats, back and forth, I decided that it was time to tell the people what had happened to me. Very quietly, I told the people that what was done by Mahishaa to Kaali had to be repeated. She desired a praana-prathishta, a consecration where the very life breath would be given to 'hold' Her.

It could never be a sacrifice, which entailed giving up something worthy in exchange for something inferior. I was privileged and ready to do it, not for Her sake, but for my own. Welfare of the people would be a byproduct. I was not going to declare, not even at the point of my death, that I was going to do this in the 'larger' interest. No. Kaali was precious to me and everything else mattered far less than Her to me.

There was total silence after my words. Then a cacophony of noise broke out. Very few people believed me or took me seriously. The majority of them mocked me. Yet, there was a skein of fear which was woven into their derision. Was there an off chance that I was right?

Silently, I sought Kaali's love and blessings as well as the sheer size of Mahishaa's love for Her. Without saying another word, I slowly displayed the right side of my body. From my neck, which I had cleverly concealed with my scarves, to that of my hip, which I had ensured that no one noticed, thanks to my self-imposed celibacy for Three months, my body was full of lumps.

It was as if each wound that Mahishaa had earned in his battle with

Kaali was blooming in me. There were times when the pain had been excruciating. I had then imagined all the weaponry that Kaali had held in each of Her Thousand arms. Had She used ALL of them on Mahishaa? I imagined Her thrusting metal into Mahishaa. All the while, he had loved Her and She was acutely aware of it. My pain of mere flesh misbehaving was hardly anything compared to that!

The crowd fell totally silent, this silence having a very different quality, all of its own. People moved away as I walked away to my car and then, home.

What followed was a huge clamour. The whole world, it seemed, loved a lover, however unlikely a one it was!

Suddenly there were huge crowds spreading stories of Love, rather than conflict. People were urging each other to think and then think differently. The media and the craftier of the priests and the politicians, tried to make me the new icon of this faith. I had no time for them. I was spending time with Kaali. The rest of the time left to me was spent in assuring those I loved that we would all meet again together, rather like Mahishaa had done with his Kaali. Love, as Kaali had told me, was indeed, immortal.

❊ MAHISHAA ❊

What a crowd-worshipping
you, love.
I smile to myself
I do not care
To look at their motives.

For this moment at least
They love you
Like a typical lover
I bask in that love!
I push my way through
Struggling to reach you
Till people see who I am.
There is a whisper
Running round
Like a Manthra
Which parted
Water bodies
On the whims of
The Gods.

I have to be there
For their Navarathri
To happen.
I have to be near you
To fight you.

You look more beautiful
Than you did
Last year.
Now you have the right
To look at me.
Not meeting
Your adversary's eye
Does not become warriors.
I gaze at you and let them think
It's the same with me.

Only Vishnu, your brother
Has damp eyes.
Did He think of His Radha
When He saw me?
Gods can't be quizzed about
Matters of
The heart, especially when
They place me as a prop to you.
I don't care!
This official proximity to you
Makes each Navarathri
A festival, for me too!

❊

Tonight my darling, I cannot sleep
It's been a week of war.
Nearness to you has been my blessing
You must either accept me
Or I forget you.

Tomorrow will be my last night on this Earth
Beautiful, for it was here that I saw you
For the very first time.
You have given me ample indications
That you would like to end it.
I gave you permission to kill me
When I realised you were going along
With what the Devas desired
Than with what you yourself probably did.

It is YOU that I am worried about
Who will you talk to, about me?
Who can understand each change in you
With each breath you take?
Who will Devi, decipher
Whether the flush on your cheeks
Is anger, strain of battle
The Sun shining directly above you
Shyness or that insidious joy
Proximity to me gives you?

Who can understand
Your silences are more verbal
Than the sounds you make
With your lips.
Darling your lips are for silences
Not speech
They are to be gazed upon
They are to be kissed
Softer and redder
If only they would bear my name once!
Just as a consolation prize for me
My love, who is sure
To kill me.

Death was an acceptable protocol of Togetherness
For a Goddess and a demon blessed
With the curse
Of loving you.

❋

Were you in repose, sleeping
And I allowed to sit by your side
I would wonder what was more beautiful
Your open eyes, or your eyes closed this way.
I would count the number of eyelashes
You have on each eye
Then I would look at the lines
On your sweet lips
Watch your bosom rise and fall
With each breath you take
And realise from where
The Seas learned their movement.

I have watched you annihilate

My Dhumravilochan, able commander
And his team with just a Hoonkaar.
Then tell me love
Why are you playing with me?

I have given you my all
The only thing left with me
Is my desire for you.
Was that wish of mine
Too useless, too unworthy for you
To deign to acknowledge
Let alone, accept?
Or is it that you realise my love for you
Is worth much, much more
Than all this put together?

Darling I have led
Such an undisciplined life
Making it easier to kill me.

Huntress are you scared to kill
The prey who stands stock still
And ready to die before you?

Why is your mercy only for those
Who worship you?
Believe me, I tried and tried
To loathe you
This is one thing I must add
To my short list of failures

On which appear
Making you care for me
If not actually fall in love
With me.

My Soul is yours, my heart too
Beloved enemy.
Let my body catch up
Is it that you will miss me
Once I am gone?
You can resurrect us
And kill me again
To the sound of the 'Devi Maahaatmyam'
Navarathri after Navarathri.

❁

You, anointed by the Devas
As worshipful
Why do you come to me
Making me look up to you
From twinkle toes
To twinkling eyes?

Why stand there silently
Eliciting from me a yearning
For which you will annihilate me
Something, you do not seem to be
Free to accept, acknowledge, cherish?

MAHISHAA

What is it that you seek from me
Dark lover whose skin is as soft as
Tonight's sky, mask for the Moon
Look in me, at me
Do you see anywhere anything
Alien to you?

They told me that
You are dangerous.
Told me to stay away.
Deafen myself to your music
Deaden myself to you.

They read out the names of kings,
Now vassals to me
Showed me the might of my army
The loyalty of the commanders
The limitless extent of my kingdom.

They sent beautiful women to me
Who took one look at me
And shrank away.
My love for you was a stake
To the vampires they had become
Accustomed to being.
Some of them had tears in their eyes
'Maharajan we are blessed
To witness that ocean of love in you
For someone so special
To be worthy of this look in your eye!'

They knew; my men knew that I was
In mortal danger
With you!
All I know, my love, is the void
Without you
That numbness far more lethal
Than that certain pain
Of your killing me.

❋

Not possible my darling
To stop loving you.

Something I hate.

Love for you has pierced me deep
With each breath of mine,
I lose more blood
From the wound you gave me
With such insouciance
That I am forced to laugh
At your temerity.

Here I am, Emperor of all domains
And a demon to boot
Women fear me, even as
They are turned on by me
They were all so keen
To capitulate.

Your rejection seemed
An aphrodisiac to my jaded senses.

Dangerous lover
Realise there is only
This much of games
Which can be played on others
I, included.

My counter-moves will be lethal
Unpredictable
I shall leave you
To be a Goddess
No doubt worshipped
But very rarely loved
With this naked passion
Which is all the worship
That I know.
All prayer I can muster
My Death endorsing
My undying love for you.

❋ KAALI ❋

Without you, Mahishaa, I can get off
My lion mount, rehabilitate it
Into diminishing forests
Where the wood is cut
For Fire Oblations to Gods.

Without you I can let fall
Those weapons honed
Against your existence.
Their metal has been warmed
To my body temperature.
My many hands unclasp
Slowly, after you are no more.
A couple of them can be used
To tie up my thick unbound hair.

I can wash off all bloodstains
Cover myself in sandalwood
I can change my burning gaze
To a benign one, or a distant one,
Something my devotees interpret
To be fathomlessness, endlessness
With these changes.

But without you, I can survive
A century or so, of Peace.
Yes, lack of that vitality
The battle held
Between you and me
Now stranger, to this non-me.

❀ **LAKSHMI** ❀

Nowadays, Kaali, only my soul
Hangs around you as worship.
Not giving you a bath
Decking you up, feeding you
The choicest items for Nivedyam.

Adorning you with flowers
Intertwined with the Nine gems
Both glowing
Richly in reds and greens
Of rubies and emeralds
And the brooding blue
Of sapphires mined
From the midnight sky.

I no longer recite
Your One Thousand names
Shlokaas in Sanskrit and in exquisite vernacular
To you.

My body that I used and abused
With meat, liquor and intoxicants
Far more sober
Than your glance.

Yes, the same one I laid
On silken sheets, rough Khadi cotton
With men and a woman or two
And a person of undecided sex
Who just wanted to be cuddled
Saying fascinating stories in return.

This body is tired, bereft of its soul.

It seems to want to reach you too
A rare succulent seasoned in the pyre
With retreating memories
The fervent prayer of my cells
Saying, 'Take me, take me now KAALI!'

❀

They called me insane
Blamed the chemicals in my brain.
They bound me in chains
Force-fed me medicines
To keep me away from you.

You were black
You were destruction
Decked in jewels
They were golden
The ones who collected accolades
Like flowers being heaped
By your feet, daily.

They were Music

MAHISHAA

Loud and rhythmic
You were melody
Unheard by all, save me.

They were the garden
With disciplined plants
With embroidered flowers,
Growing upright and straight.
You were the forest
That sheltered wild beings.

They were the canals
Where graceful yachts were tethered
You were the Sea
Humming by the shore.
They were stones, sculpted
To be buildings
You were the rocks that made harbour
For storm-tossed captains
Like me.

They were calm, Moderation
In all of their activities
You were violent in your anger
More so in your love.

You were arrogant
Calling for proof
That my love was greater
Than my life.

Ah! I was your lover, dearest
What mattered it
That it was you who hesitated?
I have enough love
For the two of us.

Come, let me drape an armful of your
Dark, fragrant hair.
Let me build myself a kingdom
Of your eyes, glances.

I have taught myself
To sleep comfortably
Near naked weapons
Bristling with thirst
For my blood.

Yes darling, indeed I have loved
And lost my reputation
My very Life!
But indeed it is for me
That I did all this.
It was to win you, my precious, true
But never for your sake
Love is never a sacrifice.
My account ledger
Still holds a huge positive balance
Alien to this unbalanced world.

Tell me something
Or if you are not happy with that
Ask yourself
Are you alive?
So, alive to feel the Cosmos
Moving in you
With its ancient movements
Choreographed by Her
That woman who makes
Everything else
Second best, almost effortlessly!

Have you loved
With an intensity
Which makes hurricanes
The breath of babies
Napping after a full feed?
Loved, like nothing else matters
Like nothing ever did
And will never do?

Ask yourself
Assassinate your insecurities
That kill you before you have lived
And from within that silence
Grow your own Love.
Live!

Kaal

This was the time that she had been waiting for, all her life.

The night seemed to be filled with darkness akin to cotton wool. She felt its gossamer presence in her lungs. The full moon was being ingested by Rahu. Before the eclipse the Moon hung fairly high up in the sky. It was a dazzling silver, blotting out all the stars. She wanted to tell the Moon to dim its light a bit, hide behind clouds and whatever it was not to draw attention to itself. Rahu was on the prowl, His phantom talons out, His red eyes spewing hatred on the Moon. She wanted to urge the Moon not to be full, to hide away in the dreadlocks of Shankara. Nobody would then dare approach the Moon!

Shankara had a way of looking at one benevolently which, however, had the effect of stopping one dead in one's tracks. She waited by the ancient doors of the Kaali shrine.

Temples were closed during eclipses. Not even a ray of light was supposed to enter the sanctum sanctorum. The ancient wooden doors fitted together snugly.

The doors of the Shri Mahalakshmi shrine were made of wood too; but they were covered with silver. Scenes from the puranic epics were etched on them. None of the poojaris were sure whether the panels in the newer temple fitted together perfectly. So they had hung an expensive sari in front of the doors. It was of the traditional length worn by Tamil Brahmin ladies and was of a deep red colour with an orange border. The gold thread worked into it had first been coated with silver and gold electroplating then done to it. Some rich devotee had given it as an offering in the Shri Mahalakshmi shrine for his daughter's marriage.

There was no one in the temple complex. Lunar eclipses scared even the guards who were supposed to be in the temple premises all night long. They compromised by locking themselves up in the Gopuram room. The eclipse would start at Nine at night and end at Three in the morning.

She looked up at the sky as she waited by the closed doors of the Kaali shrine even though it was forbidden to look directly at an eclipse. Rahu had started gobbling up the Moon so fast that He was never able to digest it. She brought both her hands to her heart.

'Kaali!', she whispered and touched the point where the panels of the door met. Silently as if the door had just been shut in the evening before, the panels swung open. There was another set of doors made of polished wood up three steps. It was pitch black inside. She was sensing her way in. Her fingertips were working like her eyes.

'Kaali!' she said again. The inner doors swung open. There at the eye level of the Goddess' idol a lamp was burning brightly. Kaali's eyes seemed to be dancing with black flames. Her hair, sculpted out of stone,

seemed to wave in the air. There was a fragrance of a thousand blooms in the shrine.

The woman knelt before Kaali. She could not take her eyes away from the Goddess' glance.
'Kaali!' she said again.

'Kaali I do not know any manthras. I do not know how to worship you. I had heard of you, how you were locked in ...as if anyone could keep you locked in... yes of course! In a heart, yes. Locked with Love. They said that you are cruel, fierce. A killer. Someone who devastates if the worship is wrong... vengeful.

But you are so beautiful! So calm. You were waiting for me... weren't you? I could sense you ...feel you. I am sorry my dearest. I am sorry. I am sorry that you were in a room, all by yourself. Nobody to see you... look after you. No! You look after us... not the other way around. I am sorry! I am sorry... forgive me that I had to behold you thus! What a sinner I am! How blessed I am to be the first one to see you in ages. Thank you! Thank you!

How long I waited for this! Here eat of my flesh, drink of my blood. I am YOURS. I am yours for all time...!'

Her hot tears fell on Kaali's feet. She felt the cool stone slowly turn into warm flesh. As she looked up at Kaali's face the Goddess smiled back at her.

'Take me to you Kaali! This world of yours is beautiful. But you are far far more so. Do not leave me yearning for you anymore. I am yours. Like that demon who chose to die rather than leave you. I too choose that. Make my choice happen O kindest of kindnesses, love of Loves, wealth of wealths. Be mine the way I am yours. Be mine for all time!'

Shri Mahalakshmi's temple and the Shri Pallikondeshwarar's shrine opened the morning after the eclipse. As it became lighter people noticed that the walls of the old Kaali temple had crumbled at night. All the stones were scattered on the ground. But Kaali stood proud and powerful, as beautiful as the day they had sculpted Her, or She had emerged from the rock.

The gathered priests, the archaeological experts and the crowds noticed one strange thing about the idol. There was a perfectly carved idol of Mahishaasura where the ground had been discoloured, as if an object which had once been there had been removed. The face of Mahishaasura resembled that of the woman. She, however, was never seen or heard of ever again.

Mahakaal

Shiva and Parvathi were relaxed in the comfort of Their home at Kailasam. Shiva was manifestly able to hold opposites in harmony at the same time. This made Him the perfect Guru, as there was no subject which was alien to Him. Parvathi often went to Him with questions meant to increase the knowledge of scholars, rather than to assuage Her ignorance. This was a definitive play between Shankara and Shankari. Very few realised the deep truth hidden in Their Divine play or Leela.

It was always cold in the snow bound Kailasa ranges. But by November, it had turned a few degrees colder. Only the locals inhabited the place. The pilgrims, trekkers, fitness experts, mountaineers and the merely curious had climbed down to the plains to return for the next season. Shiva and Parvathi were never really free of Their devotees; nor did They wish for that.

High up in the mountain, They could always drape cloud curtains around where They were. The Sun, Moon and all the stars and planets would reveal themselves or stay concealed depending solely on Their mood! This was the night after Deepavali. Parvathi had delightedly looked at the lamps lit below on Earth. She was not bothered about the reason for the celebrations. She loved its beauty!

Suddenly She turned to Shiva.

'Shiva!' She waited for a moment.

'When I ultimately killed Mahishaa, ultimately....'

She had already told Shiva about Mahishaa's Supreme Love for Her. It had shaken Her to the core. She had then felt humbled by the size of it. For days, Parvathi was pensive. She had done Her duty, but somewhere in Her was the feeling that She had been less than fair to Mahishaa. There was one question of his that She had not been able to answer to Him nor Herself later on, and She had thought about it.

'Why did you make me fall in love with you so much, SO MUCH, if you had anyway decided to kill me?'

Mahishaa's voice rang in Her ears even now. His dark face, showing red through his colouring with passion and pain was in front of Her eyes. Sometimes She was sure that She would not have been able to kill him, without being intoxicated. In fact at his very point of death he had looked directly into Her eyes blissfully. She was the one to drop Her eyes first.

He had looked so vital, happy as he died at Her hands. She had felt dead inside through all the wild celebrations of the Devas. They were rejoicing that Mahishaa was dead and that after Nine days, She had killed him in what the Devas had considered to be a fraught battle!

Parvati had never stopped adoring Shiva; nor He, Her. Ganga, Her sakhis and not even Shiva's unspoken passion for Mohini was ever alluded to. Shakthi loved Shiva. Shiva loved Shakthi. She was sure enough of Her love for Him and His for Her to tell Shiva all that happened, including Her forbidden feelings for the Bull demon.

Shiva had stroked Her hair and hugged Her to Him. Her tears left clear marks on the Vibhuthi on His chest. They had never spoken of this again.

'Shiva', She began again.... 'When I cut off his neck with my Chakra, Sunabha, out of that fountain of blood, I saw something... ...I saw you! A pure Spatika Shivalinga rose from his severed neck and entered my heart. I did not feel that it was anything new, coming into my heart. In fact, I did not feel it at all... as if it was always part of me! Why Shiva? How?'

Tears were running down Parvathi's cheeks again. Slowly Shiva reached out for Her. He held Her hand on His heart. Shiva had told Her long ago that as Nataraja, He had danced only to Her heartbeat.

He had let Nandi, His Bull vehicle, think that it was his drumbeats which led the rhythm to His cosmic dance! After births and aeons of being together, Shiva and Shailaja, which was another name for Parvathi, were as much in love as They were the night They were married. They knew each other's bodies, minds, hearts, souls. They knew how to give and take so much pleasure from each other that each time They made love, They were like young couples learning from and teaching each other.

Shiva ran His fingers through Her hair. There was no fragrance sweeter than Hers! Parvathi looked up at Him, Her eyes like two Manasarovar lakes on Amavasi. He could merge in Her, melt in Her. His love for Her was legendary. Even He was not fully aware of the depth of His love for Her. Parvathi's love on the other hand, had been blatant, open from the time She was a baby girl. She was born for Shiva and not for a moment did She forget it or hide it from others.

Shiva kissed Her eyes, Her nose, Her lips which were as soft as velvet and as smooth. Parvathi held on to Him. He was Hers.

'Shivaay!'

Shiva addressed Her by the name She loved the most.
'You saw me come out of Mahishaa's neck and enter you, right?'

Parvathi nodded, Her mind on what Shiva was doing to Her.

'Did you ever think that there was anyone, anyone at all capable of loving you more than I?'

Parvathi shook Her head.

'It was I. Mahishaa.'

Shiva kissed Her again on Her neck.

'We had to do it, my love. We had to show human beings how to love, how to fight, how to lose, how to win, how to die, how to live!'

Shiva kissed Parvathi again.

'You, my love, you have not lost Mahishaa's love, nor have you hurt him unforgivably. All through those days I watched you struggle to deny Mahishaa's love. I saw your loyalty to me. I wanted to show you, more than tell you that love is all there is. Love is the highest, the best. Love is what makes us Divinities change into human beings, demons and incarnations because Love and its manifestations are nothing but what is best in us, we who are considered to be the best! I love you too much to let you lose such a love. I love you, my darling Shakthi!'

Mahishaasura, Mahishaasuramardini. They were together always, after all.

❂ **MAHISHAA** ❂

Your Eyes, my eyes
Your Thrishul, my chest
Your Sunabha, my neck
Your battle, my love.
No Mahishaasuramardini
Without Mahishaasura.
You know what to do, do it!
I am ready.

Glossary

Aadi Amaavaasi before the beginning of the New Moon phase in a lunar calendar.

Aarathi worshipping with items of daily use like lamp, incense, cloth etc.

Amaavasya night of the New Moon.

Ammumma grandmother.

Ashtami the eighth day from the New moon sighting; towards the full moon.

Bhagavatham is the Bhagavat Geeta.

Bhaktha devotee, worshipper.

Bhakthi faith, devotion.

Dakshina alms given for religious purposes.

Devi Maahaatmyam is paens to Devi, the Mother Goddess.

Duritham burden, cross, destiny.

Ghee clarified butter.

Grantham means a religious text, book.

Harem quarters where women for sexual use are kept.

Homam fire worship; ritual of worship with fire.

Hundi is a collection box.

Id ka Chaand means the New Moon sighted in the month of Eid when the Ramzan fast is broken, after a month-long period of daily fasting. This moon sighting is considered a rarity, seen only twice in the Islamic year.

Japakusumams Japa is chanting, meditational recitations. A variety of flower used in worship, japa is called japakusum, also jabakusum. This is the hibiscus used generally in Mother

Goddess worship.

Kalpas are time cycles in the subcontinent's religious calendar. Translated as eons.

Kunkumaarchana worship with vermillion. Kunkumam is vermillion; iron oxide powder used by women to put a dot on their foreheads and in worship in the subcontinent. Also known as sindur.

Lakshmi self incarnation of the Goddess as the Goddess of Wealth, Lakshmi.
Lalitha sahasranamams a text with a thousand names of the Goddess. It is contained in the *Brahmanda Purana*.

Leela Devine Play.

Mahishaasuramardini, Bhakthavalsala, Bhagavathi, Durga, Devi, Mahamaya, Mahakaali, Kaali, Parvathi, Shankari are all names of the Mother Goddess in the Indian subcontinent. Locally, she is also called 'Mai Ma', *Ammavari*.

Mahishaa is an indigenous tribe in north Bengal and Jharkhand states of India. The lore of killing of Mahishaa, their king, represents dominance of a migrant people over local populations.

Manthras religious chants.

Matlabi opportunist.

Mhasoba is an indigenous community in west and south India.

Moksham absolution, Nirvana; a higher state of mind, liberation from mortal cares.

Mundu is a wraparound used as garment.

Navarathri nine days of festivities celebrating the Goddess's victory over Mahishaasura. In a lunar calendar, it comprises ten days of the moon's journey from the new moon to full moon phase.

Paan is a leaf chewed in the subcontinent (Piper betle), also called betel leaf.

Payasam is a milk-based sweet.

Poojari a priest.

Pooja worship.

Pottu is the dot on foreheads women put.
Pranaa life.

Prathishta is the act or ritual of establishing; a consecration.

Rahu is an imaginary planet used in astrology. Also a mythical character.

Rakthabeejaasura was a mythical demon whose every drop of blood cloned him.
He was killed by the Goddess who did not let a drop of his blood fall to the ground.

Rakthapushpanjali offering of blood to the diety; a sacrifice, human or animal.

Sakhi is a woman friend or companion.

Sanatana Dharma Post Vedic Hinduism.

Sari is a wraparound used by women.

Shankara is another name for Shiva, consort to Kaali.

Shlokas hymns.

Soundaryalahari is a religious text in praise of the beauty of the Goddess.

Sraswathi self incarnation of the Goddess as the Goddess of learning, Saraswathi.

Sunabha Shiva's bow and arrow. Also known as Pinaka.

Swami a priest or religious leader.

Tandoor is a subcontinental oven.

Tapasya penance; meditation.

Thechchi is a medicinal herb, Ixora coccinea.

Thrishul trident.

Tulsi is basil.

Vedas religious texts from the Indian subcontinent.

Veera-swargam the heaven that heroes are supposed to attain.

'*Hum*', *Aum, OM, Omkar, Hoonkaar* are the first sounds humans make O+M. They are called the primal sounds and are part of invocation songs, prayers and chants.

Acknowledgements

To

Kaali, through and beyond Space and Time.

Mahishaa for bringing a proportion to Love.

The Oceans which incubate words.

Headed by the star Karthika Thirunal Lakshmi Bayi, my beloved Ammumma, all those ancestors who continue to bless me.

Aashish, Mavis, Jagdish Shetty; Abhed Kiran Ravi Kumar Pillai Kandamath, Abjijit Panwar, Antonia Filmer (with an ancient Soul); The Chathurvedis: Arvind, Akshay, Neena and Shilpi, Arvind Kulkarni.

Anirudhdha (my brother), Rima, Meena, Kedarnath, Rhea (the Kaali filled one) and Easha Bahal, their Raju who collected Four Hundred litres of Ganges Water; Apoorv and Chinmayi Kurup and their son, Ankur Kashyap, his wife and Aarav; Anupam Lal Das (a very special 'Thank you'), his junior Anirudhdh, Vikas Verma (thanthri), Aditya Satsangi, Andreas Heitmann, Anil Kumar Vadavathoor; Anuj Bahri (who is sitting on my manuscript even today), his thoroughly gentlemanly deceased father, his beautiful wife Rajni, Mithilesh (a veritable encyclopaedia of knowledge about books), Bhaskar of Bahri Kids Section; Ayyappan, Shobha, Priyakutty, Unnikuttan, Teacher Saar, Rukmini Valiamma, Sreekumar Varma (Ammawon), Geetammayi, Vinayak Varma (artists and friends more than family) and their extended families; Aadi Keshava Sami, Dr Kannan; Rathish, ex-EO, Guruvayoor.

His Holiness the Shankaraachaarya of Shri Govardhan Math, Puri, uncompromising erudition and practice (with pranams).

The Alacode clan, especially Shailaja, Ambili who rhymes with Kambili, Aji, Kala, Chikku, Sudha, Sulu, Kunjikannan, Mohanan (planter).

The late super scholar Ajithan G Kurup, Vanajakshi Amma, Padmini Menon, Awu, Thambi Anna, Ganga, Raju, the late Deepu, the late Gopalakrishnan and extended family, Ganga, the late

Madavoor Gopalakrishnan Nair.

Balachandran (BSS), Charchavedi Babu, Professors Bindu and M G Sasibhooshan; Gautam Padmanabhan – Ramayyan, friend of Shri Padmanabha Swamy.

Bharathi Shivaji, Vijayalakshmi, Prathibha Prahlad, Geeta and Rajeev Chandran and their extended family; the late driver Chandran, Sarath Chandran and family.

Chandralekha IAS, Abhijit Iyer Mitra, son of my adopted daughter. Adopted son Subbayya Shetty.

Lawyer and dancer Ambili, Gayathri Padmanabhan (Hidimbi) and the respected Kalanilayam lineage.

Indu Varma. Kuttan.

Devi Das Gurukkal, Grisha, Bhavani and her brother, Nousha and both sides of the family.

Dili, gone to better climes.

Einar Tangen and his beautiful daughter. Sonny Badiga and his mother, wife and kids.

Naduman Ganapathi Tirumeni and family; Geeta, R Narayanan IAS, Govind, Simrit, Alina, Manju, Surjeet, Pavan and family; Karthika, Noupour (Mustafa, remember Geeta Cheriamma ?!); Pierre Audinet, the late Reghuettan, the late Vijayammayi and extended families of ALL clans here.

Gopalakrishnan C.A., Radha C.A., their son Kannan (one of the greatest readers I know).

Gopal Subramanium (true lover of Shri Padmanabha Swamy).

The Kaudiar clan especially Daddy (C R R Varma) who told me when I was Nine years old, that I would become a good writer. Ashwathi Thirunal Rama Varma and Sangeet Natak Academy awardee Gopika Varma for immersing themselves in Art.

The Kattumaadam clan: the late Kaattumaadam Kumara Swami Thirumeni (with pranams!), Eashanan Thirumeni, his mother, Srija and sons, Praveen Thirumeni, his mother, Shreedevi, Isha,

Kunju (the brilliant fruitarian, so much like his late grandfather).

Elizabeth Kuriakose, Neenu and family.

Vadakkedam Kuttan and extended family.

Prasanna Ramaswamy, Andreas Voight, Kiran Malhotra; Maya Sharma Sriram, her daughter, Madhumita Dutta, Barun, Sheila Kumar, the ever-suave Sunil, the bubbly Kelly, Kamala Eradi, Lata Rajeev (of the beautiful feet); Ratna and Krishnakumar (to whom I am Hyde and Jekyll respectively); Mohini and Rohini Gupta.

Dhanasree, her beautiful grandmother, Aparna, Bhakthi Hiranmayi, Nandkishore.

Dr Ballal, the whole Pai family, Mini's Santhosh, Priya's James, Sheela's Ikka and Shoufeela's Ashruf, Rema's Ramesh, Viju's Heman, their families; Sindhu, Beena Chakrapani, Shamla, her cousin Faisal, Kamal and families; the beautiful Sugandha Iyer; Shri, Shreya, her husband, the late beloved 'Anki' (T M Ganeshan); Padma Teacher, Deepu, Kalyani, Mahima, Hari (for books and milkshake), Manoj, Salil, their mother and families; K R Rajan, Venkanna, Othikkon Prasad, Promode Nedungadi, Vandana, Ammu, Appu, Lata Chechi, Suma Chechi and their extended families; the late Praseedam Sir, his late wife, Rajesh Kumar Praseedam, Anitha, John Sir and his sister.

Dr Maniben, Dr Rajesh (Mansi), B R P Bhaskar and extended family, the late Bindu.

Sanjay, Rhea and family.

Martin (Marty - Kutty), Sarojam Valiamma (supplier of yummy Chammanthipodi); Mini, Unni, Divya, Vidya, Hariharan and Dileep (Swastik Mural Paintings) and their families.

Radhika, Venu Chettan (Pada Veedu Kaavu) and extended family.

Rajkumari and Tucker, IAS.

Aastha and Manish from Apple Computers, especially Aastha for her courtesy and patience.

Sony, Preeth; Special special people from HDFC who treat people with a 3000 rupee account and a multi-billionaire the SAME way.

Pavan Bhushan. Marvel beyond compare.

Attingal Ranjith, Nandakumar; ex sub group officers Sasi and Nandakumar; Radhakrishna Warrier, sub group officer Vaishakh, Das, Rajeev Krishna Chaithanya (Sopaana Nriththam); Sunil,

Suresh, Vaibhav and Rahul, Raj Sadhwani, Kishore, Nafees Fazal, Hachchu, Noorie, Nishi; Tiwari of Varanasi, Tiwari of Bangalore.

Aishwarya Pandit, her parents, Karthikeya, his parents, children.

Rajan Jewellery, Pookkada Rajendran.

Jawed Habib (through hair long and short), his entire team, Beena Joykutty (Maria Rosa for my decent clothes) and her family.

Sudha Ganesh, Rameshan (Valiashaala); Madhu and Lata Ambat; Vidhubala, Jennifer Lynch, Payal Saluja, Divya Dutta and the late Irrfaan Khan.

The late Maniyammayi, the late Gopu, Suchithra, Kukku, Ammu and their extended families.

Mathur Subramaniaru, his Annapoorneshwari, Susha, husband, Shankaranarayanaru, Saju and the whole family through four generations.

Ettacode Madhu, Krishnan Thirumeni.

The Nalapat clan: (especially) Chinnen, Shodu, Devi, Chikki, Chandu, Vishnu, Deepthi, Shiv (our Nityaanand lookalike but more handsome), the star Kamala Das (Amma, for her non mother-in-law talks), the late Kalipurayath Madhav Das (Achan) Sulu Edthi, the late Unniettan (for showing me elephants on TV), his kids and grandkids, in-laws; the late Sundarettan, Vasanthettathi; the warm and loving Lynwood clan, Baby Ettan (with his famous tomato fish) and beloved beloved Balamani (for icecream and books and movies); and the late Inga Mama, the late Krishnoppu, the late Madhavi Amma and the sweet late Sharada Oppu (who loved fairy tales).

Shantha (chef par excellence and part of the family). The late Dhanalakshmi Fordyce.

Shri M, spirituality and lemon pie in the Bangalore airport. He told me that one can approach Kaali by all means, but that one should be ready to give up one's head to be a link in HER garland of skulls!

The late Saraswathi Amma teacher, who taught me my first letters; Daisy teacher, Irene teacher, Mohana teacher, Sarasa teacher, Rema teacher, Madhavikutty teacher, Suresh Sir, Gopala Raman Sir, Shivakumaran Sir, Abraham Ponnachchan Varghese Sir, Leelamony teacher, Susheela George and other lecturers of Women's College, Thiruvananthapuram; Sister Rosette and teachers of Carmel Convent; Sister Rita Maria and teachers of Nirmala Bhavan.

Police Jayachandran. Police Deepak.

Devika, Maheshwari Chechi, Nachi and his extended family.

Dr Leela and her husband Omcherry.

Ordinary Dragon Swami Hariprasad.

Dr Roxna Swamy (who may think all this to be mumbo-jumbo), Dr Subramanian Swamy (for that magical journey to Kailas Mansarovar); Geetanjali (for seeing me as I am); Chu, Maya (yet another Marilyn Monroe fan); the late Susheela Subramanian, Srikantan and Nirmala.

Padmanabha Sharma, Jathavedan, Ravindra Bhat, Mullapally Narayanan Thirumeni, Ranga Bhat, Prasad Ranga Bhat, Sreenath Panicker, Ramalinga Iyer, SS Iyer, Brahmamangalam Vasudeva Bhattathiri, Jayaraj, Pankajaakshan of Alacode, Kadookara Saji; the late Brahmamangalam Subramoni, Brahmamangalam Kailasan and team, the late Vezhaparambu Brahmadattan Thirumeni, his perfect student; Shrishankaran Thamburan, Vezhaparambu Chithrabhanu Thirumeni and extended family.

Sharavanan Thirumeni (the Mahishaasuramardini who KNOWS), his wife, the always helpful and kind Radhika and their kids.

The staff of the following temples:

Shri Vidya Rajagopalam, Mannargudi, especially Jagannath Dikshithar.

Shri Vakrakali Amman temple, Thiruvakkarai, especially Shankara Gurukkal.

Shri Attingal Bhagavathi temple.

Shri Madayikkav temple.

Shri Ambattukaavu temple.

Shri Aavanamcode temple.

Shri Kodungallur Bhagavathi temple, especially Vinesh and Santosh. Adigal and family.

Shri Kanyakumari temple, especially Suresh.

Shri Suchindrum temple.

Shri Kundaninanga temple.

Shri Thiruvithaamcode temple.

Shri Vaalvechchakoshtam temple.

Shri Saraswathi Amman temple, especially Venu.

Shri Thrippaadapuram temple.

Shri Aalampara temple.

Shri Yakshi Amman Aalthara.

Shri Pallikunnu temple.

Shri Arunaachaleshwara temple, Thirivsnnamalai especially Shri Bhaskara Gurukkal.

Shri Aadi Keshava Perumal temple, especially the old Melshanthi who was there for Perumal when no one was!

Shri Kaali Baadi temple in New Delhi, especially Nirupam Chatterjee.

Shri Kollur Mookambika temple, especially Shri Narasimha Adiga and whole extended family. His grandchildren who love elephants).

The late Kochu Babu, the greatest mahout I know; Vijayan, a close runner-up; the late Valia Babu, Kuttan, Suresh, Mahesh, Manoj, Biju, Vinod.

Dr Rajeev, who loves his patients.

Satish Padmanabhan (Outlook Magazine) for my very first publication.

Prasanna Rajan (Open Magazine - beyond words); Vijay Soni (Open Mediaworks for all the links).

Satish Ezhuntholil Kakkad, his super smart father, Thiruvaathira Mother, Divya, Devan, Devanarayanan, Satish Ezhuntholil Thirumeni's students and poojaris.

Mundanad Promod Thirumeni.

Tharananallur Uma Devi Antherjanam (a marvellous lady), her sons Satish, Kuttan and Padmanabhan, Nisha, Saji, Tharananallur Thripparayar Padmanabhan, Tharananallur Padmanabhan Unni, their extended families and P G Nair.

E P Unny.

Giri Kailas (Attingal Bhagavathi's own), Smitha, Ananthagiri, Devagiri, Varada Dance troupe.

The Haripad clan: Malathi Chechi, Mallika Chechi (for Maantheras after my paternal grandmother Shrimathi Ammumma went); Chandrika Chechi, the late Kuttettan, the late Rajettan, the late Ajan Ammavan, the late Ramabhadran Ammavan, the late Harshan Ammavan, the late Kochaniyan

Ammavan, the late Kochikaari Leelammayi, their extended families; the late Bharathi Kochamma, Anandam Kochamma, the late Sudha. Monay Dinesha, Deepu, Mangu, Gopika, Monay Ramesha (perfect artist), Geeta (Gwaay Gwaay), Aarcha, Radhika chechi, Nandettan, Nandini, Balagopal, Suresh Namburishan, Jayashri, Aparna, and extended family.

Haridas Puthuvaamana, Kripa, their sons. Himraj Dang and his daughters. Inde. Ijaaz.

Arif Mohammed Khan (who is totally spiritual beyond banalities of all religions), his wife Reshma.

Melshanthi Mani, Unnikrishnan, Shankaran, Prashanth, Madhavan. Venu Potti who trusts the elephant Kalidasan, as much as I do. Vinu Potti. Kannan, and the late Devan Potti.

Memana Thanthri and family.

Appu Maisthri, Gopan, Jose, Babu and Girish. Pappan.

The late Vinu and his beloved daughter Meenakshi, her brother, sister and her mother.

Vaasthu expert Jyothish.

Kachani Shyaamala who came to look after me when I was just seven days old. Her late son, Sanalkumaran. The late Velu. Cooks Chandran, Murali, Prabhakaran, Appu.

Leela, her late mother, her late brother Ravi and Leela's husband.

Ajayan of Shrivalsam.

Radha with golden hands, Kannan, Hari and his sister. Arun who did a wonderful job on my father.

Unniettan to all, Kalady Unnikrishnan Thirumeni (Attingal Bhagavathi's child), the late Padmini Antharjanam, his beloved mother, Aarya (Master Chef in the making), the Kalady brothers and their families, the kitchen in his illam from where Super Doshas come flavoured with immeasurable love and incomparable taste. Rukhiya (part of that homestead).

Biju, Biju, Prashanth, Yeshuraj, Shankar, Jamal Ahmed, Kannur Shyam, Negi, Avinash, Rajinder, Umaid, Vishnu, Alim who was singlehandedly responsible for my Shrishailam darshanam, Mohammed, Naanu, Kadar, Sonu who loves the mountains and knows them like his face, auto rickshaw Devaraj. Vasantha, Chandrika, Sheela, Kalpana.

T N V Iyer (who sent me to Kedarnath, Kohlapur Mahalakshmi and Mahakaleshwar temples, his beautiful and vivacious wife Trupthi; Kamakshi, Rajeshwari, her brilliant journalist son

Markandeya; T N V's late parents, especially his feisty mother.

The 2016, 2017, 2018 Kailas Mansarovar trip people.

The Carmel, Dil-Dosthies, Great Batch, Friends Forever, the Suvarna Nalapat Trust groups in WhatsApp.

The Poonjar clan: especially Mithran Namboodirippad, Bhavani Valiamma, Muththashi Amma, Usha Cheriamma, Seeri Valiachan, Nandakumaran Chettan, his lovely wife Sudha, Nikhil, incisive writer, Jaya Cheriamma, Chittappan, Nandini, Sudharma Vimala, Preman Chettan (for accommodation in Tamil Nadu) and the extended family.

The Thrippuniththura clan: especially Sundar, Sreeja, Gouri, Preetha, her parents, the late Padmini Ammumma, the late and wise Paanjaal Muththashan for partitioning his property while he was alive, his daughters, Sarita, Sasi Anna, Hari, Christina, kids, the late Mohanan valiachan; Manu, Mini chechi, Lakshmi, super reader and writer Govindan still in his teens.

Vijayambika's late parents, especially her warm, soft mother, the late Appudu, Geeta Nair's late father and late mother (whose endless servings of Chappathis and Tomato Fry have filled my stomach and heart), her late Valiamma, Rema's late father with his looooong 'Hello', her late brother Krishnan, her beautiful mother, Lata; Reshma and extended family, Vidya's late parents.

I am NOT an admirer of kids but these are wonderful human beings:

Lakshmi Varma, Girish Varma, Anand Varma, Anjana Varman, Vishnu Raamaa Varma, Gouri Varma, Prabha Varma, Rasikapriya, Abhirami Heman, Nilloufer (Ruby), Asif, Sourabh, Rukku, Kingini, Rishi, Ramya and Laavanya, herself not too fond of kids.

Dr Prabhu, Akka, Chaaya, Shaker, Pallavi, Ganga, Padmesh, Himani, Shreedevi, Jai, extended families.

The late Dr Rudrappa. Dr Ajay, Dr Abraham; Dr Shivraj who told Nalapat, 'I take your wife into the room, take her top off and squeeze her neck!' (post-surgery drain cleansing); the late Dr Shankara Pillai, Dr Indira, the late Dr Pai, the late Dr Shankararaman, the gorgeous Dr Susheela Shetty, Dr Medal Sami, Dr Titus, the super master Dr Shashikiran Umakanth (as wonderful as his name); Dr Prasad, wizard surgeon, Dr Priya, Aniket, Advaith, Dr Nandkumar Jairam, Dr Ashalatha, Dr Sumi;

Dr Ashwathi, her husband, Dr Paul, Dr Valiathan, his wife, the late Dr Marthanda Varma, Dr Bhadra Menon.

Surinder, the late Vijinder, Rahel, Sashi, Adarsh.

The late Mythri, her precious mother and family.

The staff and chauffeurs of the Taj Mahal hotel, Bombay, Old Port Road, Mangalore, Bangalore Residency Road (with Karavalli restaurant), Bangalore Airport Taj, Residency Towers, Madras, Fortune Inn Valley View, Manipal.

Satyakam, Swathi, Eashanan and the late Peter and the late Paul.

Sunil and Tomoko (adopted family), ALL those who call me 'Akka', the way I love.

These are all people who have helped me in many ways and urged me to write!

Specifically for the book *Mahishaa*:

As in everything, Kaali my Blackie.

That area outside Nalanda Bookshop, Taj Mahal hotel, Bombay, where I was truly born.

Rajan, who decades ago taught me to destroy Body - Mind - Soul - Heart dichotomies.

Jwaalaji for enlightenment (education and literally lightening some of my burdens).

Noorjehan, Noorie.

Devi and Shreshta for patiently letting Yeshukuttan give me basic computer lessons at midnight.

Madan with whom I have a love/hate relationship, recently more the former, thankfully.

Renu Kaul Verma of Vitasta Publications who believed in *Mahishaa*.

Papri Sen Sri Raman – patient and brilliant editor and writer – who ACTUALLY understood my passion. Somesh kumar Mishra, Alisha and Faiza.

Arya Praharaj for capturing my words and soul in sketches, gratis. How can I thank him enough for the understanding of even that ONE 'love, love, love' sketch!

Pankaj Shah, famous fashion photographer, for making me a zillion times better looking than I actually am!

M D Nalapat for putting up with my strangeness of habit and soul.

Most of all my Dada of the exquisite feet, who teaches me incessantly,

but claims that he learns from me.